PUFFIN BOOKS

Finn's Roman Fort

Eileen Dunlop was born and went to school in Alloa, Scotland, near where she now lives. After leaving school she studied primary education at Moray House College, Edinburgh, but is now a full-time writer. She has written thirteen novels for children; *The House on the Hill* was commended for the Carnegie Medal and *Finn's Island* commended for the McVitie's Prize for Scottish Writer of the Year. *The Maze Stone* and *Clementina* won Scottish Arts Council Book Awards. She has compiled a book of Scottish and Irish folk tales, *Stones of Destiny*, and with her husband, Antony Kamm, has written Scottish information books and compiled two collections of verse.

D1150822

Other books by Eileen Dunlop

FINN'S ISLAND
GREEN WILLOW'S SECRET
RED HERRING

Finn's
Roman Fort

Eileen Dunlop

PUFFIN BOOKS

PUFFIN BOOKS

Published by the Penguin Group
Penguin Books Ltd, 27 Wrights Lane, London W8 5TZ, England
Penguin Books USA Inc., 375 Hudson Street, New York, New York 10014, USA
Penguin Books Australia Ltd, Ringwood, Victoria, Australia
Penguin Books Canada Ltd, 10 Alcorn Avenue, Toronto, Ontario, Canada M4V 3B2
Penguin Books (NZ) Ltd, 182-190 Wairau Road, Auckland 10, New Zealand

Penguin Books Ltd, Registered Offices: Harmondsworth, Middlesex, England

First published by Blackie Children's Books 1994
Published in Puffin Books 1995
1 3 5 7 9 10 8 6 4 2

Copyright © Eileen Dunlop, 1994
All rights reserved

The moral right of the author has been asserted

Filmset in Monotype Baskerville

Made and printed in England by Clays Ltd, St Ives plc

For Alison Coutts

Contents

1 Fear Wood

'You did really well today,' said old Mrs Lochlan encouragingly, as she opened the door into the farm-yard. 'You won't have any problems at the High School if you go on like this. Just read as much as you can, and we'll have another lesson on Friday.'

Chris Cooper nodded, holding his bag between his knees as he zipped up his jacket against the wind. It was the first of August, but in Glenaire it felt more like March, with an easterly gale tearing over Corum Hill and the wood thrashing against a drab sky.

'I'll finish the book,' he promised. 'With this awful weather, and Finn away, I've nothing else to do.'

He sounded so doleful that Finn's granny smiled sympathetically. She thought that Finn and his father might have included Chris in their working holiday on the island of Hirsay, but they had wanted time on their own, which was understandable.

'Finn will be back on Saturday,' she reminded Chris. 'Only three more days.' Then, as the wind made a grab at her skirt and blew wisps of grey hair out of her bun, 'Off you go,' she added, hoping she didn't sound too eager to get rid of him.

But still Chris lingered, slowly adjusting the strap of his bag.

'Are you sure you'll be all right?' he asked. 'Dad says the forecast's terrible.'

'I shan't blow away,' said Mrs Lochlan patiently. 'I'm going to feed my hens, have my tea and put my feet up with my library book.'

The truth was that she was missing Finn a great deal less than Chris was. Living on boiled eggs and scraps of toasted cheese, she was having a pleasant, lazy time. She had written letters, knitted two-thirds of a cardigan and read ten books in nine days.

'Right. I suppose I'd better go then,' Chris said. 'Dad will come and see to the pigs later. 'Bye, Granny Lochlan.'

He ran across the yard, climbed over the gate and waved to Mrs Lochlan through the bars. When he looked back at the first bend in the track, she had gone into the farmhouse and closed the door. A chill touched Chris which had nothing to do with the weather.

For this was the moment he had been dreading, and

trying to delay by hanging about outside the Lochlans' back door. Between Corumbeg and his own home at Frandy Farm lay half a mile of lonely path, running first between high banks of heather, then through a forestry plantation aptly named Fear Wood. Chris had never been afraid there when Finn was with him, nor worse than nervous on his own. But now he was terrified. He had an enemy, and on his way to Corumbeg he had seen him among the trees. He was sure that his enemy would still be there, waiting for him to come back.

For a moment Chris hesitated, wondering whether he could go home another way. He hadn't lived at Frandy for long enough to know the country well, but he knew that if he went on down the track to the main road and walked about a mile towards the village, he could get home by skirting Yett reservoir and joining the Frandy Farm track above the Roman field. But it would take hours, and he would have to pass his enemy's house on the way. Besides, it was beginning to rain quite heavily. Better to stick to the path, he thought, and pray that his enemy would have got tired of waiting, and gone away. With pounding heart, Chris set off along the sandy path to the wood.

It was dark among the trees. The rain and the bluster of the wind ceased abruptly as Chris stepped on to the spongy forest floor, but it was far from quiet. High overhead the conifers swayed restlessly, and one

11

fright followed another as birds stirred in the branches and the undergrowth rustled and snapped. Hampered by his swinging bag, Chris ran panting, with his head down, desperate to reach the arch of grey light at the far end of the path. As he passed the place where he had seen his enemy, he glanced up fearfully – but there was no one there.

At long last, dizzy with relief, he burst out of the wood. Up ahead of him he could see his steep-roofed sandstone house, and his father's blue pick-up truck standing outside the kitchen door. Slackening his pace, Chris walked on wobbly legs up the track towards the gate. At the very instant when he stopped worrying and relaxed, his enemy emerged from behind the wall. Chris felt his throat tighten, and heard the sharp intake of his own breath.

The boy who faced him was called Andrew Aldie, and he had appeared in Chris's nightmares for almost a year. He was the bully at Chris's school, an expert in frightening people smaller and weaker than he was. Chris, who was both, was terrified of him.

Now he stood in front of the gate, a squat, flabby boy in new denims and a black leather jacket, with shiny Doc Martens boots on his very large feet. The rain had plastered his thin gingery hair to his head, and as Chris stared into his pale, expressionless eyes, he felt his heart beginning to thump painfully, and his mouth becoming dry. This was the moment he had always feared, when he would be alone with Andrew, without an adult within earshot, or a friend to whom he could call for help. Screwing up his eyes, he waited for the swing of Andrew's hard fist into his face, the pain and gushing blood which must be only seconds away. He thought he was going to wet himself with terror.

'My dad's in the yard, Aldie,' he lied desperately. 'If you hit me I'll yell, then God help you.'

He heard his own voice squeaking unnaturally, and despised himself. Again he tensed his body against the expected assault, and wanted to scream when, instead of lunging forward, the other boy stood still, whistling tunelessly through his teeth. Oh, God, thought Chris. Why doesn't he just slug me, and get it over? He could scarcely believe it when Andrew spread out his hands and shrugged his broad shoulders.

'Cool off,' he said. 'I didn't come to hit you, and I waited to give you this. It fell out of your bag when you were going to Corumbeg.'

He pulled a red plastic pencil case out of his pocket and held it out to Chris, who snatched it suspiciously. He remained on the alert, watching Andrew's right hand; he reckoned this was a trick, so that he would be caught off guard when the strike came. He was bewildered when Andrew pushed his hands firmly into his pockets.

'I'll push off, then,' said Andrew gruffly, and was half-way down the slope when Chris, dizzy with relief, managed to lick his lips and call after him, 'Thanks very much!'

'See you at the bus stop,' yelled Andrew, without looking back.

2 An Unpleasant Surprise

With tears in his eyes, Chris walked through the empty kitchen and climbed the creaking, uncarpeted stair. The house felt cold and unlived-in; it had stood empty for two years after old farmer Murray died, and the Coopers hadn't been there long enough to impress their own identity on it. Chris's parents had spent every penny they had on buying the farm, and had explained that luxuries like a new stair carpet must wait until they could afford them. Chris understood, but he couldn't help finding the isolated farmhouse depressing, especially on a day like this. It was a relief to reach his own room, and shut the door on the shadowy staircase.

Chris liked his room, and felt as secure there as he did anywhere nowadays. It was small and square, with a window opening on to an old apple orchard, and the chimneys of Corumbeg visible between two folds of moorland. Chris had helped to paper and paint it, and here he had his familiar possessions, his bed and chest of drawers from the Glasgow house, a shelf of games and the cups he had won for swimming at his last school. He had pinned posters on the walls, and propped in a corner were his skis and surfboard, now gathering dust.

In the Glasgow days, every Saturday had brought a family expedition, to Aviemore to ski, to the Trossachs to climb, to the coast of Argyll to surf and sail. But since they had come to Frandy at Easter, life was different. Saturday had become an ordinary working day for Chris's father, while his mother, tired after driving miles every day to and from her work in Glasgow, seemed content to spend her weekends reading, and catching up on paperwork at the kitchen table. She had been put in charge of her laboratory at the University, and was talking about studying for a Ph.D. They didn't neglect Chris, but they weren't very noticing people, and because they were happy, they assumed he was too. Chris didn't try to put them right. He didn't see any point.

When he had hung up his jacket, Chris unpacked his bag, putting his book and the red pencil case on his desk. Then he threw himself angrily on to his bed, still fighting tears. It was only four o'clock, but already the room was half dark. The wind was battering the tired old apple trees in the orchard, and the window-panes were dabbled with rain. It was barely ten months since the golden October when Chris had first stayed with the Lochlans, and had thought Glenaire the most marvellous place on earth. He had wanted more than anything to stay there for good, and when his parents had bought Frandy Farm it had seemed like a dream come true.

But the dream, once realized, had quickly turned sour, and one person alone was to blame. It was Andrew Aldie. Rolling over on his duvet, Chris rubbed his eyes and stared at the red pencil case. What on earth was going on? The notion that Andrew Aldie would simply do him a favour was too far-fetched to contemplate.

Chris's first encounter with Andrew had taken place last autumn, when he was staying with the Lochlans and had attended Yett School for a fortnight while his mother was away. Quickly discovering that Chris had a learning difficulty, Andrew had made his life a misery until Finn Lochlan, famously, had punched the bully on the nose. This had scared Andrew off for a while, and Chris had believed his troubles were over. But he was mistaken.

In the excitement of coming to live near his friend Finn, he had completely overlooked the fact that he could only go to Yett School for the summer term. Although he looked about eight, Chris was twelve and a half, and after the holidays he must move on to the High School at Muirs, fourteen miles away. Finn, more than a year younger, would stay behind.

Which was bad enough, but worse by far was to discover that the only other pupil moving on from Yett to Muirs this year was Andrew Aldie. That was what Andrew had been referring to when he said, 'See you at the bus stop.' He had been whispering it, hissing it for weeks before the end of term, every time he met Chris where Finn couldn't overhear. He didn't have to say any more. He hadn't forgotten the punch on the nose, and he meant to make Chris suffer because he was afraid to take on Finn. Whatever the returning of the pencil case meant, Chris couldn't believe that Andrew Aldie didn't mean him harm.

Feeling too miserable to be alone any longer, Chris got up and put on his jacket again. He thought he would go out and see how his father was getting on with whitewashing the byre. Since Frandy Farm had become his, Douglas Cooper had been like a child with a long-coveted toy. He couldn't stop gloating over it, and cleaning it, and telling people what he was going to do with it. Preparing for the livestock that would arrive next spring, he had renewed fencing and mended leaky roofs, gutted the pigsty and built a new sheepfold. His weatherbeaten face was a picture of contentment, and his son envied him.

Today, however, Douglas didn't seem as cheerful as usual. When Chris pushed open the byre door, letting the light make a watery triangle on the earth floor,

Douglas didn't throw down his brush and give a beaming welcome to an audience for his latest plans for Frandy. He merely glanced up, said, 'Hi, there,' and went on whitewashing the walls with strong, tick-tocking strokes of his massive right arm. Chris leaned against the blackened wooden frame of a cattle stall and watched him, sniffing the frail odour of hay and animal breath that lingered like a memory, years after the last Frandy cows had left for market. Until recently his father had always given Chris a deep feeling of safety. One of the most frightening things was that that feeling was fast ebbing away.

For Chris knew perfectly well what Douglas's reaction would be if he suddenly blurted out the story of the pencil case and confessed how afraid he was of what might happen on the bus going to Muirs High School. Instead of raging off to the Aldie parents to complain, Douglas would put down his brush, then hand Chris down a long lecture on the psychology of bullying. He would point out that bullies are unhappy people, so Andrew must behave as he did because he had problems too. If Chris could only show that he wanted to be friendly, even that he really liked him, Andrew would change his tune.

Chris would be reminded that it was really better for children to sort out their own problems without parents interfering, and the lecture would end on an up-beat note, with the assurance that the return of the pencil case must mean that Andrew now wanted to be friends. It would all be nice and hearty, and Chris would be left feeling a wimp. The problem, he thought bitterly, was that someone who had been as strong as a young ox at twelve couldn't begin to understand the fears of a mouse.

Still, Douglas was looking very down in the mouth at the moment, and despite his own troubles Chris felt curious. He was just about to say, 'Is something up, Dad?' when Douglas laid his brush across the mouth of the whitewash tin and turned round, a frown cleaving his dark brows.

'Listen, Chris,' he said abruptly. 'Did Granny Lochlan say that Colin and Finn would be back from Hirsay on Friday?'

'No. She said Saturday,' Chris told him. 'They're sailing to Oban overnight, and she's expecting them home in time for lunch.' He squinted through the gloom of the byre at Douglas's unsmiling face. 'What's the matter, Dad?' he ventured. 'Has something happened?'

The response was astonishing.

'A gravel pit's what's happened,' Douglas said grimly, 'or is going to happen, if something isn't done to prevent it. It's in the local paper. That guy Aldie – the one who calls his house "Pontarosa", or some damn stupid thing – is trying to get a permit from the Council to dig gravel out of the Roman field.'

Chris gaped at him, aghast.

'What?' he gasped. 'But – will he be allowed? Is the Roman field his?'

Douglas hissed through his teeth and drove his right fist hard into the palm of his left hand. It was a violent action, for him.

'It's his all right,' he replied tersely. 'Whether he gets the go-ahead to turn it into a filthy tip remains to be seen. But not if I can help it. That's why I need Colin, to help me organize the opposition. Yett people are going to have to stand together over this.'

3 What the Paper Said

When Douglas had gone off in the pick-up to Corumbeg to see to the Lochlans' pigs, Chris went into the kitchen and switched on the light. He felt cold, and shocked as much by his father's anger as by the prospect of a gravel pit at the end of the farm road. Indeed, he was rather hazy about what such a development would mean, until he saw the headline of the mid-week *Muirs Express*, which was lying on the kitchen table.

GRAVEL PIT SHOCK FOR GLENAIRE!

it said, and underneath, smaller, were two statements which explained the lines of battle to come.

ENVIRONMENT AT RISK   150 JOBS PROMISED

After that the small print became a challenge to Chris, so he took the newspaper upstairs to his room. Spreading it out on his bed and tracing the words with his forefinger, he began slowly to read.

Reading anything still seemed like magic to Chris who, a year ago, hadn't been able to read at all. Shuttling around the world with his footloose parents, he had had no proper education, and until Granny Lochlan, once a teacher, had agreed to help, there had seemed little hope for him. Now, thanks to her skill and his own determination, he was learning fast, and was pleased to find that he could make out the newspaper story pretty well. The information, he thought, was worth the effort.

Chris discovered that Mr Maurice Aldie, of La Pontevedra, Glenaire, had applied to the Regional Council for permission to excavate gravel from 2.25 hectares of land between the river Aire and the A823 road, known locally as the Roman field. There was a passing reference to the possibility that a Roman fort had occupied the site around AD 83, but what delighted the *Express* reporter was the prospect of a dust-up between environmentalists, whom he described as 'small farmers, second-home owners and Friends of the Earth', and the Council, which was likely to be impressed by Mr Aldie's promise to provide a hundred and fifty new jobs within five years. Since the two woollen mills at Muirs had closed, Glenaire was an area of high unemployment.

When he was interviewed, Mr Aldie had predicted confidently that the long-term effect on the environment would be slight. He had promised to plant fast-growing trees to shield Yett village from the excavation, and dismissed the likely outrage of his neighbours as a 'kneejerk, not-in-my-back-yard reaction'. He had stressed how much he cared for the unemployed, but wouldn't answer when asked how much money he expected to make for himself.

Chris had never seen Mr Aldie, but imagined him as an inflated version of pudgy Andrew, perhaps with a moustache like a furry caterpillar and cavalry-twill trousers instead of blue jeans. Nothing in the newspaper article made him seem any more attractive.

Hearing Shep, his father's collie, scratching and making lonely noises outside his door, Chris folded the newspaper and took the dog downstairs to be fed. As he fetched meat scraps from the fridge and mixed them with cereal in Shep's bowl, he thought what a strange day it had been – a day of Aldies, one way and another. It didn't occur to him that there might be a connection between Andrew's odd behaviour and his father's new business venture, but it was the first thing Finn thought of when he heard the story on Saturday evening.

4 Supper at Frandy

'Well, it's obvious, isn't it?' said Finn, putting his booted feet on Chris's desk and stretching out comfortably in his friend's armchair. 'He's got wind of this gravel pit, and knows he'll come in for flak, the same as his dad. So he wants to suck up to us, hoping we won't be as foul to him as he's been to us. All of a sudden, big Andy needs chums. Stands to reason. Think about it.'

Chris, who was sprawling on the bed with his thin fingers wrapped round a can of Coke, thought about it, and rapidly concluded that Finn was right. It couldn't be a coincidence, surely, that on the very day when the gravel pit story broke in the *Express*, Andrew Aldie had come, all meek and mild, to return the pencil case.

'Over my dead body,' he growled.

'Over your dead body, what?'

'Over my dead body that pig will ever be a chum of mine.'

'Right on,' grinned Finn, pulling the ring on another can.

At seven o'clock on Saturday evening, Finn, his father, Colin, and Granny Lochlan had arrived at Frandy Farm for supper. Finn and Colin had got back earlier in the day from Hirsay; they were weather-beaten and full of tales about the fortnight they had spent on the island, far out in the Atlantic, helping to rebuild the village which had been abandoned more than sixty years before. It should have been a happy reunion of friends, but no sooner had they all sat down at the kitchen table than Douglas, his enormous body taut with anger, launched forth about the gravel pit. Scowling blackly, he ranted until his food was cold about the greed and selfishness of Mr Aldie, and what must be done to stop him turning beautiful, unspoilt Glenaire into an industrial wasteland.

'If you draft a letter to the Council, Colin,' he said, 'we'll call a meeting at the Jubilee Hall at Yett, and get everyone to sign it. Copies to our Member of Parliament and as many environmental groups as we can think of. And we'll get a committee together to organize resistance. God, it doesn't bear thinking about,' he added, bringing his fist down so hard on the pine table that the cutlery rattled. 'The noise and the dust, and

26

filthy trucks thundering up and down the glen. We can't let it happen.'

Colin and Bess, Chris's tiny mother, chimed in indignantly, while Granny sat glowering into her fish pie. Finn, watching her across the table, couldn't help being amused. He was as furious as anyone about Mr Aldie's plan, but he was pretty sure that Granny was glowering in opposition to the general mood. It was touch and go, he thought, whether she would suddenly howl the others down and say her piece, whatever it was, or go into one of her huffy silences which might last until this time tomorrow. Finn was fond of Granny, but she was not, as strangers sometimes imagined, a dear old soul.

Eventually she exploded. Thumping the floor with the walking stick she had taken to using to draw attention to her plight as a rheumaticky, overworked old lady, she cleared her throat loudly.

'And what about the one hundred and fifty jobs?' she demanded raucously.

An uneasy silence fell. Finn watched his father's thick black moustache beginning to twitch, and waited for him to snort, as he always did when somebody disagreed with him. He was careful not to look at Chris, whose giggling at the snorts was very infectious. Suddenly the snort rang out like an elephant's trumpet; Chris snickered and pretended he was blowing his nose. Fortunately nobody noticed.

'Now you listen to me, Mother,' began Finn's father furiously, but Granny was into her stride now.

'No! You listen to me, Colin Lochlan,' she interrupted, thumping the floor again. 'And the rest of you had better listen too. I don't know this man Aldie, and you may be right in saying that all he cares about is money. And of course it's sad that a beautiful place should be scarred, even partially destroyed. But there are a hundred and fifty jobs at stake, for pity's sake, a hundred and fifty new starts for people who otherwise may never work again. My father lost his business in the 1930s, and my husband was unemployed when I met him. I know how having no work depresses people, and eats into their self-respect.' She looked round the ring of startled, pained faces and sighed wearily. 'All I'm saying is that there are different kinds of destruction,' she said in a quieter tone. 'Go ahead and save your glen if you can. But remember that there's a price to be paid for everything.'

In the uncomfortable aftermath of this speech, the boys excused themselves, collected Coke and biscuits, and went upstairs to Chris's room.

'Is she right?' wondered Chris, as he switched on the light and the electric heater.

Finn shrugged.

'You have to choose,' he said. 'I think the environment matters more.'

'So we're going to help Dad and Colin?'

'Sure,' assented Finn, then spoiled his environmental zeal slightly by adding, 'It isn't as if the Aldies are mates of ours.'

Which was when Chris began to tell him the story of the pencil case.

5 About Romans

Having ruined the evening, Granny was very cheery on the way home. As the old grey Land Rover sputtered along the deserted main road and rocked slowly up the long, uneven ascent to Corumbeg, she plied her son affably with questions about the Roman field. Had there ever been Romans in Glenaire, she wanted to know. Were there any excavations? Or was it a case of, 'Well, it's possible, but . . . '? Colin, who was not best pleased with his mother, answered at first in gruff monosyllables. But he had been a teacher of Latin before he became a farmer, and eventually his own interest got the better of his irritation.

'It's certainly possible,' he conceded. 'When the Roman general Agricola invaded the Highlands in AD 83, his strategy was to plug the glens with forts, trapping the native Caledonians in the mountains to the north. Remains of forts have been found at the entrances to Strathearn, Glenshee and Strathtay, among others.'

'What about Glenaire?' asked Granny brightly, while Finn, slumped on the back seat, wondered why his father could never mention the Romans without sounding as if he was back in front of Class 2A. Still, this was interesting.

Colin braked suddenly to avoid a small, startled rabbit caught in the headlights' beam. Determinedly ignoring Granny's annoyed tut-tutting, he changed gear and proceeded more cautiously.

'Glenaire was on Agricola's route,' he said, answering her question, 'so it's reasonable to suppose that the same thing might have happened here. The place they call the Roman field would have been an ideal site, high and level and in a loop of the river. But it hasn't been excavated, so there's no proof, one way or the other.'

Finn could scarcely keep his eyes open. He had been up at dawn after a night spent on board a boat tossing on the Altantic, and it was far past his usual bedtime. But he was sufficiently awake to take in what was being said, and as the Land Rover juddered to a halt on the cobbles outside the kitchen door, an idea suddenly occurred to him.

'Dad,' he said, stifling a yawn. 'I was wondering. Wouldn't it be a good idea if somebody did excavate the Roman field? I mean, if they dug up some really interesting Roman things, maybe the Council would refuse to give Mr Aldie a permit. If the field was important for history, you know.'

Colin switched off the engine and the lights, plunging the yard into total darkness.

'That's a good thought, Finn,' he said. 'Unfortunately archaeologists have never shown the slightest interest in digging here, and without some real evidence to encourage them, it's unlikely they ever will. No, Douglas is right. It's far better for us to play the environmental card. Kick up a fuss about damage to the landscape, loss of wildlife habitat – that sort of thing.'

Since Finn had only recently taught his father the difference between a gannet and a herring gull, he detected some insincerity in this sudden concern for wildlife. It went through his mind that a man who was always quoting Roman poets ought really to care more about Roman remains. But he had never won an argument with his father yet, and anyway, at the moment, he was more interested in a thought of his own.

'Yes, but just supposing somebody did find something Roman?' he persisted, tussling with the broken handle of the door.

Colin was learning to be patient with Finn.

'I should think it would make a difference,' he admitted. 'But time isn't on our side. We have an excellent case, but if we start making a Roman fort part of our objection, the Council will accuse us of stalling, and be more likely to ignore us. These people aren't interested in the Romans, Finn. They're interested in appearing concerned about unemployment and getting themselves re-elected.'

'Don't provoke me, Colin, please,' said Granny sharply in the dark.

6 A New Daydream

In the morning, Finn woke with a sense of being in a
strange place. For two weeks, he had opened his eyes
at dawn in a narrow ex-army bed in the old school on
the island of Hirsay, and lain listening to the sounds
of wind and sea. He hadn't been alone, for there were
twenty-five other people on the island, helping to
rebuild the ruined church which Finn's grandfather
had attended as a boy. The walls were now up, and
the next group of volunteers would help to raise the
roof. Finn had had a wonderful time, and he was
already looking forward to going back next summer,
to attend the first service to be held in Hirsay church
since 1929.

But he was glad to be home, too. Lying in his own
bed in the morning light, he let his eyes run over
familiar objects and linger on the map of Hirsay

pinned to the wall. It had been made before he ever went to the island, and it made him smile now, a map embellished with imaginary features, a haunt of pirates and sinister Blue Men. Finn had outgrown it suddenly, but not the habit of imagining himself a hero in exciting and improbable situations.

Now, as he recalled last night's conversation about the Roman field, the first scene of a new drama began to unfold delightfully inside his head. Closing his eyes, he visualized himself standing in the Council Chamber at Muirs, where he had once been on a school visit. He was wearing a smart jacket and trousers, and across his palms lay a burnished Roman sword.

'You can't give Mr Aldie a permit,' he was telling the astonished councillors imperiously, as he held out the sword for them to see. 'I have discovered a hoard of Roman treasure . . . '

This pleasant daydream was interrupted by a sharp knock on his bedroom door.

'Chores!' called his father's voice, and as the large feet clattered away downstairs, Finn pushed back his duvet and climbed out of bed.

It was a beautiful morning, still and cool, with the sun like a pale orange lantern on the eastern sky. But the forecast was, as usual, poor. Enjoying the new closeness to his father which their shared holiday had brought, Finn helped to open the henhouse and carry buckets of swill to the sty, where three jolly pigs were eagerly awaiting breakfast. Finn leaned over the wall, watched their huge behinds playing boomps-a-daisy as they jostled for position at the trough, and went on with his daydream. By the time he had swept the yard and fed Gruach, the year-old collie pup, he was in front of the television cameras, shaking hands with the director of the museum chosen to display his finds.

After breakfast, Finn thought, he would cycle over to Frandy and have a talk with Chris. He could see that this daydream, like the old one about Hirsay, might run and run. But it had also occurred to him that this one had a better chance of becoming reality – given some resourcefulness and a lot of good luck.

Chris was kicking a football about in the yard when Finn arrived, and ran to open the gate for him. Finn propped his bike against the wall, and the two boys sat down on the bench outside the back door. The sun was burning through a thin veil of early mist, and only a purplish line along the western sky warned that by evening the weather would be foul again.

'I thought,' said Finn, wasting no time getting to the point, 'we might go down to the Roman field this morning and have a look round.'

'What for?' asked Chris, who had a spider on his finger and was trying to tickle it into running up his arm.

Finn explained.

'Dad says no one knows whether there really were Romans in Glenaire,' he said, 'because archaeologists

36

are too dumb to come and find out. But if Roman things were found, Aldie probably wouldn't get his permit to dig gravel out of the field. So I thought we might have a look.'

'What for?' repeated Chris, still playing with the spider. He had seen the Roman field from the road, an unremarkable, roundish platform of tussocky grass, dropping away sharply to the river on the far side. 'There isn't anything to see, is there?'

'Well, I'm not sure, really,' admitted Finn. 'But there might be some ridges or hollows in the ground, like in those aerial photographs Mrs Ritchie showed us at school. Then at least we'd have an idea where to start digging.'

The last word seemed to hit Chris's head like a falling stone.

'Digging?' he squawked, letting the spider escape in his fright. 'We can't dig there. It belongs to Aldie, for God's sake!'

It was Finn's turn to look amazed.

'Cool it, man,' he said. 'I'm not saying we should hire machinery. I just think we should go down this morning for a look-see, then we can work out what to do next. OK?'

Chris didn't think it was OK at all.

'I don't rate that idea, Finn,' he protested. 'Suppose big Andy sees us? He'll tell his dad we're trespassing, and there'll be a terrible fuss.'

'Ach, to hell with big Andy,' replied Finn robustly.

'I thought we'd decided he was trying to suck up to us? Anyway, he'll be at church just now. Oh, come on, Chris!'

So Chris came on. He didn't want to set foot in the Roman field, or anywhere else connected with the hated name 'Aldie'. But he always did what Finn wanted in the end, because being Finn's friend was the most important thing in his life.

They freewheeled down the hill together on Finn's bike, Finn standing on the pedals and Chris on the saddle, his thin legs sticking out on either side. He didn't have a bike of his own because his parents hadn't allowed him to cycle in the city, and now a shortage of cash meant that he must wait until his birthday in December. Below them they could see the Roman field on the other side of the main road, screened by a brake of spruce from the garden of the Aldies' house, La Pontevedra. It was customary in Yett to sneer at La Pontevedra, a huge, ranch-style house surrounded by emerald lawns and named after a place in Portugal where the Aldies had a holiday villa. Before the Aldies came, a derelict farmstead called Clayrigg had occupied the site; the Aldies had not been forgiven for demolishing Clayrigg, though no one in their right mind would have wanted to live there. Finn began to pedal as they passed the gate, a high rustic archway with 'La Pontevedra' burned into a section of log, suspended from the crossbar on two chains.

'I just hope they don't keep Rottweilers,' muttered Chris, not meaning to be funny.

But Finn laughed as he leaned the bike against the fence. Under the glassy, disapproving stare of Mr Aldie's sheep, the boys climbed the gate, scrambled up the banking and set off across the Roman field.

You could see, as Finn pointed out, why it would have served the Romans' purpose well. A flat-topped knoll with clear views up the glen, the field was protected round most of its circumference by a loop in the fast-flowing river Aire. Finn explored with his toe various ridges and depressions in the grass, but admitted that it was impossible to know whether they were natural features or not. Chris grunted moodily and kept glancing nervously over his shoulder towards the road.

At length Finn led the way into a copse of skinny grey oaks, clinging to the very edge of the field. Wind and rain had exposed roots like rheumatic old fingers. Here, high above the tumbling green water, there were signs of activity, marks of tyre-treads in the grass, white pegs hammered into the loose, gritty earth.

'This is where he's going to start,' said Chris.

'If he gets a permit,' Finn replied.

The boys sat on the high edge of the bank and shared a bar of chocolate which Finn had in his trouser pocket. There was sun and a stiff breeze, and a view across a valley so wild and green that it was hard to believe humans had ever inhabited it.

'It reminds me of Hirsay,' said Chris, as he watched a kestrel hovering above its small shadow on the hillside.

But Finn's mind was on the Romans.

'We could dig here,' he said. 'Nobody would see us from the road, and the ground's so soft it would be easy. Dad says it'll be weeks before the Council decides about the permit,' he added, forestalling an obvious objection.

'Why here?' asked Chris, with the tired air of someone who knows he is being talked into something.

'There would have been a stockade along the top of the bank,' persevered Finn, trying to recall the little he had learned about the Romans two years ago at school. 'There might be bits of stake buried.' But then, catching Chris's sceptical eye, he let the truth come tumbling out. 'Oh, come on, Chris. Let's have a go, just for the hell of it. Think how marvellous it would be if we did find something, and saved Glenaire from a yucky gravel pit. We'd be on the telly, and we'd do big Andy in the eye. One coin or a piece of pottery, that's all we really need. I know it's a long shot but we might be lucky, and at least we'll have some laughs.'

Chris didn't think he'd be much amused. He knew it was scarcely worth it, but he made one final effort.

'I thought we were going to help your old man to paint Corumbeg,' he said.

'Mornings,' Finn told him as he wiped his chocolatey fingers on the grass. 'Mornings we'll be painters. Afternoons we'll be archaeologists. OK?'

'Yeah. OK,' agreed Chris, giving up. 'We'll have to look out for big Andy, though.'

'Ach, forget big Andy,' advised Finn easily.

7 Two's Company

Although just for a second he felt like pushing him over the high bank into the river, Chris didn't really blame Finn. He knew that Finn believed he had dealt with the problem of Andrew Aldie, once and for all, ten months ago. Finn would have been horrified to learn why forgetting big Andy was something Chris couldn't possibly do. He would immediately have offered to punch Andrew's nose again, which was the last thing on earth Chris wanted. Chris was grateful to Finn for standing up to Andrew on his behalf, but the chief reason he hadn't told him about Andrew's recent bullying was that he couldn't bear to have the incident repeated. Much as he liked and admired Finn, he couldn't help occasionally feeling envious of Finn's strength, and humiliated because he was hiding behind a boy who was more than a year younger than he was.

Alone and kicking his ball again in the afternoon, when Finn had gone to Muirs with his father to buy paint for the house at the Sunday market, Chris went on thinking gloomily. If ever there was to be a solution to his plight, he knew he would have to work it out for himself. But one solution just wasn't on, he told himself, slamming the football viciously against the stable door. He would never make friends with Andrew Aldie. If the returning of the pencil case was, as Finn thought, a sign that Andrew wanted a truce, he could forget it. After all he had been through there was no way, Chris swore, that he would grovel and grin and pretend friendship just because, for the moment, Andrew needed mates. I may be a wimp, he thought sourly, but I'm not as big a wimp as that. Besides, he'd still beat me up on the Muirs bus, the first day he felt like it.

Towards evening the sky darkened, and rain fell gently all through the night. Waking occasionally, Chris was comforted by its unemphatic patter on the roof; rain tomorrow would delay the time when he had to trespass in the Roman field. So he was disappointed, at half-past seven, to see a thin lance of sunlight dividing his bedroom curtains, and to find, when he got up, that the night clouds had parted on a washed green and blue morning. Already steam was rising from the grass in the orchard, and Chris didn't need Finn, exuberant on the telephone at five to eight, to tell him that it was going to be a beautiful day.

'We can't paint because Dad has to go to Muirs to see a man about a ram,' he said, 'and Granny's going with him to shop. So it'll be a good opportunity to nick spades without having to answer snoopy questions. What else do archaeologists use?'

'God knows,' grunted Chris, but accepting the inevitable, went on, 'If Dad says it's OK, I'll come over when I've had my breakfast.'

Douglas promptly said that it was OK.

'I'm going to Edinburgh this morning to talk to a man at the Scottish Environmental Forum,' he told Chris. 'Then in the afternoon I'll have to start whipping up support around Yett. Granny Lochlan will give you a bite of lunch, and I'll be back about teatime.'

Chris put a spoonful of cereal into his mouth, and watched his father padding abstractedly around the kitchen. He was fond of Douglas, but knew that, with a brand-new bee in his bonnet, he would be a fairly half-hearted parent for some time to come.

The saddest thing, Chris reflected as he ran through the wood, was that this was life as he had yearned for it. In the city winter he had dreamed of waking at Frandy on a perfect summer morning, and Finn ringing up to discuss how they would spend the day. Despite his anxiety he couldn't help noticing the fresh tang of wet spruce, and the clearness of little streams bubbling across the needly forest path. A pheasant broke from the undergrowth in a whirl of metallic green, and as he came into the light Chris saw a lark rising, a tiny, tuneful speck on the sky. Everything was as it ought to be, outside his own sad heart.

Finn was in the yard when Chris climbed over the gate, tying two rusty spades on to his bike with a length of cord. On the cobbles he had laid out two trowels, a ball of string, a groundsheet and a roll of plastic bags. On the doorstep were two cans of Coke and two small packets of ginger biscuits. Because they emphasized his partnership with Finn, all these pairs of things pleased Chris. But that didn't stop him saying grumpily, 'It's going to be a damn nuisance, hauling all this clobber up and down the hill every day.'

Finn shook his head.

'Not so,' he replied, as he began to stuff his bits and pieces into two carrier bags. 'I found the trowels and spades in the hayloft. They must've belonged to the guy who lived here before us, and Dad won't even know they exist. We'll hide them down at the Roman field. Oh, and by the way,' he added, straightening his back, 'you'll be glad to know we don't have to worry about a visit from big Andy today. He's gone to Perth to get his new school uniform.'

Chris stared.

'How do you know?' he demanded. He was about

to say, 'Fraternizing with the enemy?' but managed to stop himself in time.

'They were there when I went down to Yett post office to get the newspaper,' explained Finn. 'Andy and his mum and his wee sister. Mrs Aldie was telling Mr Clark that they were away to Perth to get Andy's new uniform. Then wee Goldilocks piped up that they were going to have lunch at Pizzaland and go swimming in the afternoon. OK?'

'Very OK,' agreed Chris, but then some foolish, unworthy twinge of suspicion made him want to ask, 'Did you speak to Andy?'

This time he let the words come out. Finn gave him a withering look and rolled his eyes till the blue almost disappeared.

'Why would I speak to Andy?' he replied. 'He pretended he was looking in the shop window, and I pretended he wasn't there. Have you got your new uniform, by the way?'

Chris wished he hadn't asked, and when he heard the answer, so did Finn.

'I've got the shirts and a school tie. But they're having to order a blazer and trousers from somewhere in England, because they didn't have any small enough.'

'Take the bags,' said Finn hastily. 'I'll push the bike.'

8 Three's a Crowd

Chris was certainly relieved, when they got to the Roman field, to know that Andrew's large person wasn't going to loom suddenly out of the trees. Even if trouble was only shunted into tomorrow, he had a breathing space today. Finn didn't bother to conceal his bike, but padlocked it to the gate. Together the boys carried the spades and bags over the damp, humpy grass.

'I asked Dad last night about Roman forts,' remarked Finn, as they relaxed on the groundsheet after their exertion. 'He thinks the fort guarding a glen like this would have covered about two hectares of land – roughly the size of this field with its edges squared off. There would've been an earth wall with wooden palings on top, and barracks for about five hundred men. A cohort, which was one tenth of a legion.'

Chris grimaced at him.

'Are you really interested in all that guff?' he asked, helping himself to a biscuit.

Finn shook his head. He had always been interested in the past which he could reach through his grandfather's memory, the family past of island life seventy years ago. But the great company of invaders, who had followed their standards through his land and disappeared into the mist nineteen centuries before he was born, meant nothing to him at all. His only concern was with what they might have left behind.

'You know I'm not,' he said. 'I'm interested in finding something which will put an end to Andy's dad's nasty little money-spinner.'

'Such as?'

Finn shrugged.

'I'm not sure,' he said. 'Dad says that at other forts near here they've found broken pottery and glass. And coins – that sort of thing.' He wasn't going to tell Chris about his dream of finding something really spectacular. That would be a wonderful bonus, if it occurred. 'All we need,' he stressed, 'is one small thing to prove there were once Romans here. After that, archaeologists will be queuing up to do the work for us.'

Chris gave one of his grunts, and watched

the shadow dappling of oak leaves on the khaki groundsheet. He had always been bored stiff by the Romans, aggressive busybodies in silly clothes, who seemed to do nothing but invade countries that didn't belong to them. But he needed to be with Finn, so he got up, and patiently held the string while Finn marked out a line where he thought the stockade must have been.

'We'll move the turf first,' decreed Finn, 'about a metre on either side of the string. Then we'll dig down and see if we strike anything.'

The rational part of his mind told him how improbable this was. Buried wood disintegrated, and finding a Roman coin, or even a shard of smoky grey glass, could only be the greatest good luck. But Finn believed in luck, because he reckoned he had been lucky before. Chris didn't, but he took up a spade. When Finn started hacking at the grass, so did he.

Even where the soil was friable, lifting turf was far from easy. All morning the two friends chopped busily with their spades, and often resorted to tearing up chunks of grass with their bare hands. By lunch time their fingers were sore and their nails broken, and there was little to show for their trouble. Still, neither felt inclined to abandon the job. Finn, developing his dream of fame as Scotland's youngest archaeologist, scarcely noticed the discomfort, and Chris found that physical effort stopped him thinking at all. He liked the smell and texture of the red earth with its scurrying insects and pink worms, and for three hours Andrew Aldie was absent from his mind.

After soup and sandwiches at Corumbeg, the boys returned to the field on the bike. Their technique gradually improved, and in the afternoon they achieved twice as much as they had in the morning.

It was twenty to five when Finn glanced at his watch and said, 'I think we should pack it in now, Chris. I've got my evening chores to do, and Granny will be ratty if I'm late. Where do you think we should hide our gear?'

Chris wiped his forehead on the back of his wrist and looked around.

'Under that clump of gorse would do,' he suggested, pointing to a patch of dark shrub.

'True,' agreed Finn. 'We'll put the small stuff in the carriers and weigh them down with the spades. Then –'

He stopped abruptly, and Chris at once knew why. It was like feeling a cold shadow falling over their backs, however impossible that really was. But certainly they knew, before they turned round, that they were going to see Andrew, his heavy body encased in stiff denim and his round, expressionless face crowned with hair like orange wool. Chris swore violently under his breath, and Finn whistled in annoyance. But there was nothing they could do.

'Hi, Andy,' said Finn unenthusiastically, while

Chris did his rabbit-meeting-snake impersonation. 'I thought you were swimming this afternoon.'

Finn realized that he had miscalculated the time you needed to stuff your face at Pizzaland, splash with your little sister in the beginners' pool and drive back from Perth.

Andrew seemed uninterested in what Finn thought. For a moment he stood under the trees, his blank eyes surveying the bared earth and the tools the boys hadn't had time to conceal. Finn waited to see what would happen next. He was surprised.

'I saw your bike at the gate,' Andrew said eventually. Then, 'Are you digging for Roman treasure?'

There seemed no point in denying it. Finn nodded.

'Mn. I'd thought of it myself,' Andrew said. There was an awkward pause, then he continued, 'This is my dad's field, you know.'

Here we go, thought Chris, seething with barely concealed loathing. Now for the accusations of trespassing, threats and gestures of menace. But again, what happened was unexpected.

'Will you let me join in?' Andrew asked. 'Please,' he added, causing Finn to gape in astonishment.

Chris was gaping already.

'What'll you do if we say no?' inquired Finn, when he had partially recovered. 'Tell your dad?'

Andrew frowned.

'Don't know. Maybe,' he said. 'I just want to join in.'

For Finn, it was a delicate moment. On one hand, he could feel waves of dissent and resentment emanating from Chris, and smelt trouble ahead. On the other, he knew that a rejected Andrew would certainly tell his father, and the excavation would be stopped before it had properly begun. Involving Andrew would shut his mouth and if, Finn thought unkindly, the boy was too pinheaded to understand that he was helping with something designed to ruin his father's plan, that was his problem. Finn was going to dig in the Roman field, whatever the cost to anyone else. So, ignorning Chris's frantic body language, he said casually, 'OK. Two o'clock tomorrow, and you'll have to bring a spade.'

Chris never saw the pleased, faintly pathetic smile that appeared on Andrew's unattractive face. With one wordless look of betrayal at Finn he threw down his spade, grabbed his jacket and ran out from the trees. Sobbing, he stumbled across the grass, climbed the gate and made for the Frandy road. The only clear thought in his mind was that he would never speak to Finn Lochlan again, as long as he lived.

9 Falling In

'You're unusually quiet this evening,' remarked Granny, as she and Finn fed the hens together before supper.

They both liked eggs, but shared a distaste for hens, with their quivering wattles, cross faces and pushy manners. For a moment Finn watched the clumsy birds pecking jerkily at the feed, then he confessed.

'Granny, I've fallen out with Chris.'

He thought she would be annoyed. The two families of Corumbeg and Frandy had become very close, and Finn knew as well as anyone the debt his father owed to Douglas for helping him to become a good farmer. But Granny seemed unconcerned.

'Oh, I see,' she said calmly, picking up a tin basin containing a few smeared eggs. 'Well, you'll just have to fall in with him again, won't you?'

Remembering Chris's scarlet, furious little face, Finn reckoned this might be more easily said than done.

Still, 'Am I allowed to go over and fall in with him after supper?' he asked.

He thought he would feel more comfortable if he had at least tried to put things right.

Granny hesitated, and Finn knew why. She was still finding it hard to break the fearful, protective habit she had formed when she was bringing him up on a Glasgow street. She kept telling herself that here in the country children were safe from muggers and louts spoiling for trouble, and had allowed Bess to persuade her that there was no need to keep tabs on the boys during the day. But after supper, with night drawing on . . .

'You may go,' she compromised, 'but Dad will drive over and bring you home. I don't want you out alone when it's getting dark.'

Finn didn't feel even a twinge of irritation. This was what he had been used to, all his life.

There was never much meal-time conversation at Corumbeg, and as he ate his sausage hotpot Finn thought hard about how best to smooth Chris's ruffled feathers. Finn liked Chris, but there were things about him he found difficult to understand, such as his possessiveness and his unwillingness ever to forget the past. If he had known about Chris's recent trouble with Andrew he would have felt differently, but as it was he thought his friend's behaviour in the afternoon childish and stupid. He doesn't have to act wee just because he is wee, thought Finn self-righteously, avoiding the fact that he hadn't behaved particularly well himself. But by the time he had finished his second helping he had decided what to do. He swallowed his yoghurt, said goodbye and ran through the wood to Frandy, under a vast peach moon.

Bess was in the kitchen, doing something complicated on her computer by the window.

'Chris in?' asked Finn, putting his head round the door.

'Upstairs. Sulking,' responded Bess, sounding completely indifferent to this state of affairs.

She peered at the screen and tapped a key. The computer beeped and the image rearranged itself. Finn withdrew his head and climbed the stair.

Chris was lying on his bed, holding a comic in front of his face. He had recognized Finn's step on the uncarpeted treads.

'Push off,' he ordered, as Finn opened the door. 'Push off, get lost and drop dead.'

Finn ignored this unpromising invitation. He crossed the floor and sat down in Chris's armchair. Chris immediately flounced over and studied his comic with his face to the wall.

'You could let me explain,' suggested Finn.

'I don't want you to explain. Go away.'

It had been a long, tiring day, and despite his desire

to be friends again, this pettishness was too much for Finn. He got up, went over to the bed and tweaked the comic out of Chris's hand.

'Now, will you listen?' he growled.

It might have made things worse, but it didn't. Chris rolled over, glared and made an unsuccessful snatch at the comic. Then he collapsed like a burst balloon.

'Oh, all right,' he muttered, and Finn sat down again.

'OK,' he said. 'Get this into your skull first. I don't want Andy Aldie hanging around any more than you do. He's no mate of mine, and he never will be.'

'Then why did you say he could help us?' demanded Chris, with a spurt of indignation.

Finn sighed.

'Because we've got to play him along. Oh, can't you see?' he coaxed. 'If we don't let him join in, he'll tell his dad, and bang goes our chance of digging for Roman remains.' Then, knowing that this outcome would be less distressing to Chris than to himself, he put on a conspiratorial grin. 'But if we do find something,' he went on relishingly, 'just think what hell he'll get from his dad for helping us to scupper the gravel pit! I reckon he'll knock Andy's block off, don't you?' He knew he was appealing to Chris's worst instincts, but told himself it couldn't be helped. When he saw a slight, appreciative smirk on Chris's face, he pressed his advantage. 'Besides, if Andy's there, you – I mean

56

we won't have to worry all the time about him jumping us. Could be a good thing, really.'

Chris ran his fingers through his spiky brown hair. He knew he was being wheedled, but he was realistic. He didn't want to prolong the quarrel, and he knew that Finn would never abandon his digging plan. That being so, he saw sense in what Finn said. It was unlikely that Andrew would attack him when Finn was there, and having the bully in view, however unpleasant in other ways, would be better for his nerves. And if Andrew did get into trouble with his father, that would be as good as revenge.

'Well, all right,' he said grudgingly. 'Just as long as he never gets to imagine he's a real mate.'

Finn, who had got everything he wanted, was careful not to let his triumph show.

'Do me a favour,' he said, shrugging dismissively. 'He's an outsider. Always will be.'

He knew that this was what Chris wanted to hear. Yet as he spoke, Finn couldn't avoid a vivid recollection of Andrew in the Roman field that afternoon, pink with pleasure at the news that he would be allowed to join in. But just as he had succeeded in suppressing pity then, Finn succeeded in suppressing guilt and self-reproach now.

10 The Outsider

Since April, Colin and Finn had been working just as hard to restore Corumbeg as Douglas had to restore Frandy. Together they had rebuilt walls and repaired fences, hung gates and laid a new concrete floor in the pigsty. Douglas had helped them replace cracked window-panes and mend the farmhouse roof, and now repainting the shabby old buildings was the one big job that remained. They had chosen cream paint for the walls and green for the woodwork, and only Granny was tactless enough to suggest that with a gravel pit to windward, it might have been more sensible to choose grey.

'There isn't going to be a gravel pit,' Colin and Finn told her in unison, to which Granny replied, 'Huh? Hm.'

So, determinedly optimistic, Finn and Chris donned

old clothes and spent a few fine mornings helping Colin to slap fresh paint on to the peeling walls. It was hard work but good fun, and even Chris managed to enjoy himself a bit.

Normally Douglas would have been helping too, but he was out and about trying to drum up support for the 'Save Glenaire' campaign. Bess had made posters inviting everyone to attend a crisis meeting in the Jubilee Hall on Friday at 7.30, and Finn and Chris had coloured them with fluorescent felt pens. It was all quite exhilarating, and the boys, rushing round in the car with Bess to pin up the posters in the village, had enjoyed the feeling that they were fighting a battle on the side of right. So they were upset, on Thursday, when Douglas turned up at Corumbeg for morning coffee with a tired expression on his lined brown face.

'I'm not doing as well as I'd hoped,' he admitted, when they were all seated round the table with their coffee mugs. 'I've been to see the minister and the doctor, and that retired headmaster down at Burnside, but they all made excuses. Said they were too busy to sit on any more committees. Mr Curtis at Middle Corum never seems to be at home, and the farmer at Netherhope is away at an agricultural fair.'

'What about the village people?' Colin asked.

Douglas tutted peevishly.

'Oh, them! All ready to grumble, but not to stand up and be counted. That about sums it up,' he said bitterly.

59

Finn could see how disappointed he was, and wanted to say something heartening.

'Maybe they're just shy,' he ventured.

'Maybe they're just feeble,' retorted Douglas.

But Colin, who wasn't famous for optimism, for once took a more hopeful line.

'I think Finn's probably right, Doug,' he said. 'We can't judge our support till after the meeting. None of these folk wants to be the first to speak out, but they'll back us up when they're all together. You'll see.'

Later on, Finn would remember that Granny had looked up from her knitting and given Colin a peculiar look. He saw her open her mouth, then shut it again, which was most unusual.

'Has Bess had an answer from Mr Aldie yet?' Finn wanted to know.

Bess, as acting secretary of the campaign, had written a letter to Mr Aldie, inviting him to come along to the meeting and defend his plan. Douglas shook his head, and when the conversation turned to farming matters, the boys went out again to the yard.

'All the same, I wonder if he will come,' said Finn, dipping his brush in the tin of paint.

'We can ask his precious boy. We see him often enough,' replied Chris waspishly.

Finn groaned inwardly. This was not something he needed, or wanted to be reminded of. Andrew had come punctually to the Roman field on Tuesday and on Wednesday, and would no doubt come again today.

He must, Finn thought, have a hide like a rhinoceros, for Chris's determination to show him that he would never be a real mate was absolutely ruthless. Every lunchtime Chris seemed to put on resentment like a poisoned coat, and as the three boys worked his small body was surrounded by an almost visible aura of hostility. Andrew, again surprisingly, seemed to accept the situation, working doggedly under Finn's direction and rarely opening his mouth.

When Finn decreed that it was time for a rest he came and sat silently on the groundsheet; the first day he had tried to share his cheese snacks, but after Chris had rudely refused, didn't offer again. Finn, who had been determined to get his own way but now didn't like paying for it, was appalled by the dire atmosphere, and also by the failure of his attempts to get a conversation going.

'Have a good time at the pool, Andy?'

'Nope.'

Andrew was not an accomplished swimmer.

'Get your new school uniform?'

'Nope. They didn't have a blazer big enough.'

If only Chris had come in here with his own school uniform story, Finn thought, they might have had an ice-breaking laugh together, but Chris merely looked contemptuous. It was OK, suddenly, to be too puny and wee, but not OK to be too large and over-developed.

Andrew did come on Thursday, and again on

Friday, the day of the meeting at the Jubilee Hall. By the end of the afternoon, the area which Finn had marked out was cleared for digging, and no one could deny that Andrew had done more than his share of the work. But nor could anyone call what he was doing 'joining in'. He couldn't possibly be enjoying himself. So why did he come? The only possible answer was that he still wanted friends in the event of a storm. But if so, surely he must realize by now that he should have looked for them elsewhere.

On Friday afternoon, curiosity about what Mr Aldie had in mind finally got the better of Finn. As the boys were hiding their tools in the gorse at half-past four, he asked casually, 'Is your dad coming to the meeting tonight, Andy?' although he was pretty sure what the answer would be.

Andrew, who was bending down to tuck in a corner of the groundsheet, straightened up slowly and stared at Finn. His face was already red with sun and exertion, but still its colour deepened. The pale blue eyes, however, gave nothing away. He shook his head.

Finn spat on his filthy hands and rubbed them on his handkerchief. He kept his eyes on Andrew's face.

'Ah. I just wondered,' he said. 'Chris's mum wrote to him, you see, but he didn't reply.'

He was careful not to sound belligerent, but his words were challenging, and he knew how dangerous it could be to put pressure on Andrew. He was alert to protect himself if Andrew suddenly lunged. But instead of reacting aggressively Andrew frowned, and sucked his bottom lip. Then he made his longest speech of the week.

'My dad says he isn't on trial, and he doesn't have to explain himself to anybody.' Then, before Finn could expostulate, he added in a rush, 'Look, I'm sorry about this. I don't want a filthy gravel pit here either, spoiling the environment and ruining the glen. But it's his field, and he doesn't take orders from me, for God's sake.'

He sounded so sincere that Finn couldn't help being impressed. But when he said so on the way home, Chris was scornful.

'Sincere?' he sneered. 'How can a snake be sincere?'

Finn could think of no answer to this question.

11 A Village Meeting

The Jubilee Hall at Yett stood in the middle of the main street, a grey, vaguely churchy building erected more than a century ago to mark fifty years of Queen Victoria's reign. It shared a small garden with the war memorial and a flowering cherry planted by the Prince of Wales, and it was the centre of village life. Every sort of meeting took place there, and Douglas reckoned that he had been lucky to hire the hall at such short notice on a Friday evening. It was only available because the Army Cadets were away at camp.

Although they had been disappointed when their fathers had said they weren't allowed to sit on the platform, Finn and Chris had been looking forward to the meeting. Despite Douglas's unpromising start they were convinced that, once Glenaire people had actually heard him speak, they would happily appoint him their leader. Finn could imagine Douglas at the head of a great, enthusiastic protest march to Muirs Town Hall, with a colourful banner proudly carried by himself and Chris. His only regret was that Mr Aldie had been too cowardly to appear and face the music.

'He'd have been made mincemeat of,' said Finn confidently. 'That's why he's running scared.'

'You bet,' Chris agreed.

It was left to Colin to appear twitchy as the Corumbeg Land Rover drew up outside the hall at seven o'clock, with Granny looking regal in the front passenger seat. He switched off the engine and sighed with relief when he saw that there was already a string of cars parked in the road.

'It's vital we get a good turn-out,' he said. 'We need as many signatures on that letter as possible.'

If this was a hint to Granny, it went unheeded. Before Colin could get out and open the door for her, she was stumping up the path.

Finn said hastily, 'Good luck, Dad, though I don't suppose you'll need it,' and scuttled after her.

In the cool, vaulted interior of the hall, wooden benches had been laid out, and Finn saw with pleasure that they were already quite well filled. Douglas, unusually wearing a tie with his checked shirt, was on the platform, arranging papers on a table. He looked up, grinned and winked at Finn, who gave him the 'thumbs-up' sign. He was delighted to see Douglas looking cheerful again. Colin, in the dark suit he used to wear as a teacher, went on to the platform, while Finn went with Granny to join Bess and Chris in the back row.

'Thought we'd sit here so that we could case the audience without turning round,' said Bess, who was also looking relaxed.

She seemed to be dressed for combat, in green corduroy trousers and a terrible khaki jersey. Finn thought that Granny, in her best suit and buniony but well-polished shoes, looked positively smart beside her. He scrambled over Bess's booted feet to reach Chris, who was lounging on the small of his back and sucking a lollipop.

Granny creaked on to the bench and arranged her bag and stick. She glanced around her in a bright, beady way, then watched sardonically as Colin walked solemnly down the hall to arrange a copy of his letter, pens and extra sheets of paper on a table in the porch.

'He should have been an undertaker,' she said.

'Are you going to sign the letter, Frances?' asked Bess, trying not to laugh.

Granny's snort was worthy of Colin.

'I,' she replied, 'have promised to keep my mouth shut this evening. In return, my son is kindly allowing me to follow my conscience in the matter of the letter.'

'No wonder you're in a bad mood,' said Bess placidly.

More people drifted into the hall, chatting and waving to their friends. Finn recognized Mr Curtis, the farmer from Middle Corum, the Clarks from the post office, Mrs Ritchie and Miss Barry from the school. But then, since Chris seemed to be snoozing, he let himself drift into his daydream. There had been dramatic developments, and the youngest archaeologist in Scotland now had his own television programme, *Finn Lochlan Investigates*. He had investigated the Romans, then the Vikings, about whom he knew even less, and now was introducing film of himself diving for sunken treasure in Tobermory Bay. He was enjoying this when suddenly Chris poked him in the ribs.

'Look! There's big Andy!' spluttered Chris indignantly.

Finn returned abruptly from the television studio.

'Well, stone me,' he said.

On the other side of the hall, Andrew and his mother were settling into seats about half-way down. Andrew was wearing his posh leather jacket, but it was Mrs Aldie who stood out in the crowd. A tall, handsome woman with immaculate make-up and fair hair, she was dressed in a purple suede skirt and a gold silk blouse, and carried a black leather bag on a gold chain.

'Like a swan in a duckpond,' said Bess, without rancour. 'I admire her nerve.'

Granny opened her mouth to reply, but at that moment Douglas rose and knocked with a small hammer on the table. The babble of voices died away.

12 Crisis

Douglas had nothing to say in public that Chris and Finn hadn't heard at least twenty times in the last ten days, but he said it well, and with self-control. Believing that this was his great opportunity to inspire the community with his own passionate concern for the environment, he listed earnestly the reasons why Mr Aldie's plan was against the public interest – damage to the landscape, pollution of the river, destruction of species, the ruin of a way of life which, once lost, was gone for ever. Finn felt proud to be his friend.

Next Douglas called on Mr Colin Lochlan to read the letter of objection which they proposed sending to the Regional Council, and Finn was torn between pride in his father and embarrassment at his twitching moustache and wobbly Adam's apple. Douglas then said that he hoped a committee could be formed to coordinate opposition, and urged everyone to sign the letter as they left the hall. Finally he invited discussion, and sat down.

It was a competent performance, and deserved a warm round of applause. The faint, sporadic clapping disappointed Chris and Finn, although they failed to see it as a sign of trouble to come. Even when Finn saw some members of the audience nudging one another, he felt more irritated than alarmed. In the silence that followed, Douglas and Colin drank water and shuffled their papers. The hall clock struck eight. As the last stroke died away, a wiry, red-haired man in a green padded waistcoat rose slowly near the front of the hall.

'Ah, Mr Curtis,' said Douglas, with some show of relief.

The farmer of Middle Corum was an important man in the district, who never tired of reminding his neighbours that there had been Curtises in Glenaire since the seventeenth century. The audience became expectant, but Mr Curtis took his time.

'Mr – um, Cooper,' he said, after he had turned to survey the benches with his small, pink-rimmed eyes. 'Mr Cooper, I'm sure I speak for – almost – everyone here when I say that I agree with everything you have said. However, I should like to ask you a question.'

'Certainly,' nodded Douglas courteously.

The farmer's voice hardened suddenly.

'Who gave you the authority to call this meeting?'

Finn heard Granny sigh, but his eyes were fixed on Douglas. He knew that Chris too was on the alert. A faint flush had risen on Douglas's weatherbeaten cheeks, but he answered Mr Curtis calmly.

'I didn't see it in terms of authority, but as a matter of need,' he said. 'I saw a task which I felt should be tackled with speed, and since I have few commitments at present, I decided to tackle it. I've worked in many parts of the world with environmental problems, and I thought my experience could be useful here.'

The silence in the hall was now so deep that Finn could hear a bird singing outside in the memorial garden. His eyes flickered between the platform, where his father was beginning to writhe, and Granny's face. She had the look of someone watching a play, interested but detached, as if she already knew what the end would be. Finn remembered her strange expression in the kitchen yesterday, when Colin had suggested that Yett people would back the campaign once they got together. He began to worry seriously.

Mr Curtis again rose to his feet.

'No doubt, Mr Cooper,' he said smoothly, 'you have learned much from your worldwide experience.' Then he put the knife in. 'What a pity you've learned so little about democracy. We have an elected parish council here in Glenaire, sir, of which I am chair. We have already met to discuss a response to Mr Aldie's deplorable plan. Call us old-fashioned, Mr Cooper, but we don't take kindly to smart-alecky outsiders coming here and telling us how to run our affairs.'

'Hear, hear,' somebody shouted, and the silence was at last ended by thunderous applause.

Douglas had recently shaved off his beard, and now his face had a naked, vulnerable look which upset Finn, who thought he was wonderful. But Douglas concealed his pain bravely.

'Mr Curtis,' he said. 'If the parish council wishes to organize resistance to Mr Aldie's plan, that's fine by me. But I do wonder why – if my calling this meeting was so offensive – so many people have turned out to it.'

'To see you getting your come-uppance, mate,' shouted a gleeful voice, causing laughter and more applause. Mr Curtis grinned triumphantly.

'The mean old bastard,' snarled Bess, who hated swearing. 'He had this all planned.'

'I hate these people,' whimpered Chris, but Granny nodded gravely.

The play was proceeding as she had expected. Only it was not over yet.

Almost before the laughing had stopped, a young woman seated in front of the Aldies leapt to her feet. Finn recognized her as Mrs French, the mother of one of his classmates from the tiny modern housing development at Yett Wood. Her face was blazing with indignation.

'Mr Chair,' she began in a high voice. 'I have never in my life heard such arrogant, brazen remarks as Mr

71

Curtis's. He's a fine one to talk about democracy! No one who hasn't lived in Yett for donkey's years has a chance of being elected to the parish council, and those who are have to do whatever Mr Curtis says. Why do you think there are hardly any young people here tonight? It's because newcomers to Yett don't see any point in coming to meetings. I applaud you and Mr Lochlan for trying, but you'll get little support from this bunch of toadies.'

It was the word 'toadies' that did it. Immediately there was pandemonium in the hall. Nobody bothered to address Douglas, who sat looking stunned, while Colin went red and white by turns. Villagers were on their feet shouting about slick willies from Glasgow who thought they could teach their grannies to suck eggs, while the tiny contingent from Yett Wood bawled that it was their community too. Mr Aldie and his gravel pit seemed to have been forgotten; the meeting was now about something else. Finn and Chris were wide-eyed with horror, while Bess sat with her head in her hands. But Granny sat upright, watching the fray with her birdy brown eyes.

'I'll tell you something,' said Finn to Chris, as he observed his father stressing out on the platform. 'When I get home, I'm going straight to bed.'

'Under the bed's where I'm going,' said Chris fervently.

Eventually, like all storms, this one blew itself out. A hostile silence replaced it, in which Douglas rose and brought his ill-fated meeting to a close. No one could deny that he did it with dignity.

'This,' he said, 'has been the saddest night of my life. Mr Lochlan and I wanted only to help a community threatened by catastrophe. All we seem to have done is to expose divisions at a time when we should all be standing together. We wish the parish council well in its campaign, but –' his jaw set stubbornly '– we still intend to send our letter to the Council. We hope that some of you at least will add your signatures to ours.'

He then declared the meeting over.

Because it took Granny so long to collect her belongings and rise stiffly to her feet, most of the overheated audience had poured out from the hall before Finn and Chris reached the door. After all that had happened, they didn't think they could still be surprised by anything, but they were wrong. In the porch, where Colin's letter still lay on a small oak table, Andrew Aldie was having a furious row with his mother. Andrew, bright red and on the verge of tears, was trying to get hold of a pen, while his mother, clearly upset, was doing her best to stop him.

'I want to sign it,' Andrew was panting, shaking off his mother's hand. 'Leave me alone, Mum. I want to sign.'

'For heaven's sake, Andrew!' said Mrs Aldie furiously. 'Haven't you humiliated me enough for one night? Stop making a fool of yourself, and get to the car!' There was a scuffle as Andrew made a last frantic grab at the pen, but Mrs Aldie, who was a large, strong woman, took him by the collar and pushed him hard towards the outer door. 'Get to the car,' she repeated, between her teeth.

Then, while Chris and Finn stared disbelievingly, Andrew burst out crying. His mother ran after him as he fled sobbing down the path to the road.

13 A Dismal Weekend

The next two days were so ghastly that even Chris would have been thankful to escape to the Roman field. Unfortunately another weather change made this impossible. By Saturday morning the sky had disappeared under a soft unfurling of rain, and the wind seemed to moan in sympathy with the sad souls of Frandy and Corumbeg. Only six people had signed Colin's letter as they left the hall on Friday night, and the 'Save Glenaire' campaign was in ruins.

Granny couldn't resist announcing that she could have told them how it would be; she knew all about country ways from listening to Grandpa talking about Hirsay. But who would pay attention to an old woman? She then decided to have a bad attack of rheumatism, and retired to bed with four murder mysteries and a hot-water bottle. While Douglas, Bess and

Colin relived their humiliation in each other's kitchens, drinking coffee and shuddering about the future, Finn and Chris took refuge in the Frandy stable.

'Dad's in an evil mood,' remarked Finn, as they barred the door behind them. 'Not snorting funny, snorting dangerous.'

'Sure,' nodded Chris. 'My pair are hyperventilating with rage. It's because they've been made fools of, and they don't know what to do next.'

'So they reckon Mr Curtis set them up on purpose?' asked Finn, who, in spite of the evidence, still found this almost beyond belief.

'Too ruddy right, they do,' Chris assured him. 'Dad says that's why he could never find old Curtis at home all last week. He was out organizing his own kind of campaign, the mean skunk.'

Finn shook his head.

'But why?' he said.

Through the gloom of the old stable he saw Chris lift his thin shoulders.

'Like he said at the meeting,' he replied. 'We're outsiders, that's all.'

Finn, who had so readily called Andrew Aldie an outsider, found that he didn't at all like having the word used to describe him.

But meanwhile time had to be passed, and because his recent visit to Hirsay had reminded Finn of an old pirate game they used to play, he suggested to Chris that they should play it again now. Chris agreed, and they had a fine time swinging on ropes from the rafters and walking the plank into a heap of very unsavoury straw. When they got tired they sat on an old horse blanket in the hayloft. It wasn't long before talk turned to Andrew Aldie's extraordinary behaviour at the Jubilee Hall. Chris, as usual, already had his mind made up.

'I don't think there's any mystery,' he said. 'Big Andy knew that so far his sucking up to us hadn't worked – giving back my pencil case and not telling his dad what we were doing in the Roman field – that sort of thing. Then when he heard what people were saying about his dad at the meeting, he panicked and thought he'd better make some big gesture, like signing the letter when his mum didn't want him to. I bet he reckoned when we saw his signature we'd say, "Well, fancy that! Dear old Andy's a good egg after all." It's simple, really.'

It went through Finn's mind that maybe Granny should stop teaching Chris to read out of *Boy's Own* annuals which had belonged to Colin when he was young. He was beginning to sound quaint.

But what he said was, 'I don't think it's that simple, Chris.' He looked pensively out of the window at the drifting cobwebs of rain, then went on, 'What I can't understand is why he and his mum were there at all. Andy said in the afternoon that his dad didn't feel he had to explain to anybody, and you'd think the last thing Mrs Aldie would've wanted was to go to a meet-

77

ing where she was bound to hear people saying foul things about her husband.'

'Maybe her husband sent her as a spy,' suggested Chris, 'so that she could report back what happened. Just the sick sort of thing he would do, if you ask me.'

'Mn. I suppose that's possible,' mused Finn. 'Except that I got the impression it was Andy who had dragged her along.'

'How so?'

'Well, don't you remember?' Finn said. 'When they were fighting in the porch she said something like, "Haven't you humiliated me enough already?" Andy had behaved O K during the meeting, so she couldn't mean he'd shown her up. I think she meant he'd forced her to come and hear people being vile about his dad.'

'Well?'

'Well, if that's what happened,' said Finn soberly, 'it seems an awful length to go to, making your own mother suffer so much, just to suck up to two guys you know don't even like you.' Finn couldn't remember his mother, who had died before he was two, but he knew how despairing he would have to be before he could treat Granny so badly. Then he let dangerous words come out. 'Unless he's genuinely desperate to make a new start with us, I mean.'

He saw his companion's jaw tense suddenly.

'Let's play pirates again,' said Chris coldly, and leapt through the trapdoor into the straw.

So they played, and Finn, who knew by now that where Andrew was concerned Chris was beyond reason, said no more. But now that he had started asking himself questions about Andrew, he just couldn't stop. And the more he thought, the more it seemed to him that his first idea, that Andrew wanted friends because he was afraid of flak, must be hopelessly wide of the mark. Andrew seemed to have been shrugging off unpopularity for years, so why should it matter to him now? And if, for some reason, he did want mates, why pick on such an unlikely pair as Chris and himself?

Finn didn't know the answers to these questions. But, throughout the long, dismal weekend, he was troubled by snapshot memories of Andrew. Andrew standing in the Roman field, as pleased as Punch because he was allowed to join in. Andrew saying with simple sincerity that he didn't want his father's gravel pit either. Andrew crying in the hall porch because his mother wouldn't let him sign the protest letter. It would be stupid to pretend that the swaggering bully of Yett School hadn't changed, and Finn, who had so casually mollified Chris with the assurance that Andrew would always be an outsider, now felt uneasy in his mind.

Indeed, by Sunday evening he had got to the point of being really sorry for Andrew, but sadly this decent feeling only posed another problem. Pity, Finn quickly realized, wasn't the same as liking, and he didn't actually warm to Andrew any more now than he had in the past.

14 Unexpected Invitations

By Monday morning the rain had cleared, though the sky remained overcast and the wind blustered unpleasantly through the glen. Because it must, life got back into its normal tracks; Bess went off to work, Douglas drove over to Muirs to see the bank manager about his overdraft, and Colin resumed the painting of Corumbeg. But the tired tetchiness which had replaced the fighting spirit of the previous week remained, as Finn discovered when he asked, 'What are you and Douglas going to do now, Dad? About the campaign, I mean?'

Colin, whose last brushful of paint had just dripped on to the kitchen window, scowled in annoyance.

'For God's sake, what can we do?' he snapped. 'Curtis has got us over a barrel. End of story. Don't be such a fool, Finn.'

Though it was a long time since Finn had been called a fool, he shrugged off the criticism just as he always had in the past. But when Chris suggested playing pirates instead of going to the Roman field in the afternoon, he shook his head firmly.

'We mustn't waste any time,' he said. 'It sounds as if Dad and Douglas have thrown in the towel, and we can't trust old Curtis and his gang not to make a mess of everything. So now saving Glenaire really depends on finding something Roman, doesn't it?'

He couldn't help imagining the headline in the *Muirs Express*:

YOUNG ARCHAEOLOGIST SAVES GLENAIRE!

and thinking what a sweet revenge it would be for the mortifying report which the paper had printed on Saturday, headed,

VILLAGE SNUB TO CITY CONSERVATIONISTS.

But Chris only grimaced and said, 'I suppose so.'

Finn had been reading a book called *Archaeology in Britain*, which he had found in his father's bookcase. It had a chapter entitled 'How to Dig'.

'You have to divide the site into sections,' he told Chris, helping himself to some of Mr Aldie's wooden

82

pegs and unwinding his ball of string. 'Then when you've made a grid, you dig over one section at a time.'

Chris huddled in his jacket against the wind, and glumly watched Finn hammering in pegs, stretching string between them and cutting off the ends with a penknife. When the unturfed rectangle had been divided into eight large squares, he picked up his spade and began resignedly to turn over the damp, crumbly soil.

For the rest of the afternoon, the boys worked in silence. Finn was fed up, exasperated by Chris's lack of zest for something which he thought so important. Chris, as usual, was brooding about Andrew Aldie. He had been rattled on Saturday by Finn's suggestion that Andrew might really want to make a new start in friendship; he simply couldn't believe that, whatever Andrew might say now, he wouldn't show his true colours again when they met at the bus stop. But to his old hatred and distrust of Andrew was now added a new fear, that his enemy might drive a wedge between himself and Finn.

Finn was the only real friend Chris had ever had, and he didn't want to share him at all, but the idea of making a threesome with Andrew was more abhorrent than any other sharing could have been. He watched Finn jealously out of the corner of his eyes, and wondered what he was thinking.

By half-past four they had unearthed a crow's skeleton, several lemonade bottles and a rusty tobacco tin.

'Not a lot there, unless the Romans smoked shag,' said Finn wryly.

Chris responded with a grunt.

Andrew did not appear that afternoon, nor on Tuesday, nor on Wednesday. At first Finn and Chris thought he must be lying low after his performance on Friday night, but when they saw that the gates of La Pontevedra were padlocked, they realized that the Aldies had gone away.

Chris couldn't resist saying, 'Good riddance to bad rubbish.'

Then on Thursday something unexpected happened.

'There's a letter for you, Finn,' said Granny, thumbing through a pile of mostly junk mail which the post office van had just delivered to the back door. 'An electricity bill for your dad, and a letter for you.'

Finn, who had just finished his breakfast, raised his eyebrows in surprise. The only mail he ever received was a few Christmas cards and a gift token from Auntie Phyllis on his birthday, which was in July. He picked up the thick cream envelope which Granny pushed over to him, and stared at the undistinguished writing.

'Who on earth do I know in Edinburgh?' he wondered, peering at the postmark.

'Open it and find out,' suggested Granny, pouring herself another cup of tea. 'Maybe it's an invitation to meet the Queen. The envelope's grand enough.'

The postmark was a red herring, and it was not an invitation to meet the Queen. But it was an invitation, and one from the Queen could scarcely have amazed Finn more. In the envelope was a gold-edged card, on which was painstakingly written:

Andrew
requests the pleasure
of Finn's company
at his birthday tea
on Saturday 17 August at 4 p.m.
R.S.V.P.
to La Pontevedra, Glenaire.

'Oh, no,' groaned Finn, his blue eyes circular with horror. 'He must be off his trolley.' And as Granny leaned over and plucked the card out of his fingers, 'I'm not going. No way,' he vowed.

'Oh yes, you are,' Granny said.

Everyone said that Finn looked like his grandpa, but when he and Granny were glaring at each other there was a strong resemblance between them. Before the glaring could advance to argument, however, the telephone rang. It was Bess, impatient and very late for work. Apparently Chris's invitation had also arrived.

From where he sat at the table, staring mutinously at the card and wondering whether he dared tear it up, Finn heard the high-pitched quacking that was Bess on the telephone. He couldn't make out her words, but there was no mistaking the determined tone of Granny's replies.

'Yes, of course, Bess. I do agree. Whatever quarrel the parents have, it shouldn't be allowed to affect the children. When I think of the state that poor little boy was in at the hall last Friday night . . . Oh, it's Chris howling, is it? I thought it was somebody playing the bagpipes. No, Finn isn't pleased either. Well, you'll just have to be firm, my dear. I intend to be, believe me.'

Finn, who had never in his life got the better of Granny, felt his heart sink. He put up a token fight, but he wasn't surprised when, twenty minutes later, he found himself sitting with a pen in his hand, taking dictation from Granny.

'Finn will be delighted to accept . . . '

He had told Granny that he didn't want to go to La Pontevedra because he didn't like Andrew, and because Chris would behave badly and embarrass him. He had been tempted to add that he couldn't see why he should suffer because Granny was feeling bad about Andrew, but hadn't dared. Yet he knew that none of these reasons really explained the depth of the reluctance he felt.

At the weekend, alarmed by his own feelings, he had decided as severely as he could to give Andrew the cold shoulder. He was afraid that if he didn't keep the other boy at a distance, pity would get the better of him, and make him behave in a kindly way. That

86

would be a terrible mistake; it would give Andrew the idea that Finn wanted friendship, and unpleasantness was bound to follow. Andrew would be hurt and resentful when he learned the truth while Finn, who liked to feel good about himself, would be left feeling a toad. But how on earth could you cold-shoulder someone if you were forced to go to his house, meet his family, guzzle his cake and sing, 'Happy Birthday to You'?

As he licked the flap of the envelope and stuck it down, Finn didn't know whether he was more fed up with Andrew or with himself. The whole business was a bore. But as he took the letter down the hill to the postbox, he found himself wishing fervently that Andrew would do something really hateful, as in the past. Finn badly needed a new excuse for walking away from him once again.

15 The Birthday Tea

It was one of life's mysteries, Chris thought, why he was always sent to have a bath before a party or a visit to the doctor, whether he was dirty or not. But at three o'clock on Saturday, as he soaped himself in the ancient tub that was Frandy's answer to the Aldies' jacuzzi, he wasn't pondering the mystery very deeply. Andrew's birthday party was only an hour away, and after two days of strife and torment, Chris was completely worn out. Bitterly he recalled his parents' pained, bewildered faces.

'Why are you behaving like this? It's only another kid's birthday tea, for God's sake.'

That was Douglas, who, since the disaster at the Jubilee Hall, had become glum, sulky and very, very irritable.

'I know you don't like the boy, but if he's invited

you to his party he must like you. You saw how upset he was after the meeting at the hall, so plainly he knows what's right, even if his father doesn't. Why can't you show a little kindness and sympathy?'

That was Bess, who was feeling even worse than Granny Lochlan, because she had conveyed her own dislike of Mr Aldie so forcibly to Chris.

Of course, they thought he didn't want to go to the Aldies' because of the conflict over the gravel pit, and, in occasional moments of reason, Chris saw their problem. They didn't know that he was the victim of Andrew's bullying, so naturally they thought he was over-reacting. The worst moment had come that morning at breakfast when, after two days of sulking, snivelling and whining, 'I want to go back to Peru,' he had at last tried to tell them the truth. He had scarcely been able to believe it when Douglas angrily lowered the *Independent* and said sharply, 'That will do, Chris. Don't start making up stories. You're going to the party, and that's that.'

Then Chris had seen that he was completely alone. He knew that Finn was tired of him, because he had seen it in his eyes. Now his own parents had turned against him. As he got out of the bath and dried himself, he was still reeling in disbelief. Whatever the reason for this hateful invitation, Andrew Aldie would be waiting at the bus stop, and there was no one to turn to now. In a daze Chris went to his room and put on a T-shirt and a clean pair of jeans. He picked up the birthday present which Bess had tied up for Andrew and went downstairs. Without going into the kitchen to say goodbye, he left the house and walked down to the Frandy road end, where he was to meet Finn.

It was a pleasant summer day, with birds riding the breeze and the hills stippled with the shadows of shifting cloud. Finn, with a 'Let's get this over' expression on his tanned face, was sitting on the fence by the cattle-grid. He said 'Hi' as he jumped down, but when Chris didn't answer fell in silently beside him. Carrying their birthday presents they crossed the road and walked up the Aldies' drive, like mourners at a funeral.

'Who else do you think will be coming?' asked Finn as they approached the house.

'No one. He only wants to suck up to us,' was the sour reply.

La Pontevedra was even grander close up than it looked from a distance, with heavy flounced curtains at the windows and cast-iron lamps on either side of the front door. There was a fountain in the middle of the lawn, and Mrs Aldie's Volvo estate car was parked on the pink paving which ran along the front of the house. The double garage was open and, both boys noted with private relief, empty. If Mr Aldie was off somewhere in his Porsche, there would be one less horror to face. Chris watched Finn ringing the bell, and waited with thumping heart to see who would open the door.

It was opened by Andrew, wearing checked trousers and a red shirt and looking – Chris thought shifty, Finn thought scared. The one sure thing was that his eyes had acquired an expression, and it wasn't a confident one. He licked his lips nervously and said, 'Um, come in.'

Finn and Chris stepped off the posh patterned tiling of the porch on to a green carpet so deep that the pile came half-way up their shoes. The house was silent. As Chris had predicted, they were the only guests.

Finn said, 'Happy Birthday,' and held out the box of toffee which Granny had made.

Chris, whose tongue was pressed against the roof of his mouth, said nothing, but parted with his present, a pack of felt pens in recycled giftwrap, tied with green string.

'Thanks,' Andrew said. He didn't open the parcels, but laid them on a table at the foot of the stair. Then he said flatly, 'You can watch a film or play computer games.'

Again, Chris stood dumbly, but Finn reckoned that a film would be the wiser choice. The dearth of party spirit would be less obvious if everyone was slumped in an armchair, staring at a television screen. But just as he was about to answer, the scene suddenly changed. A door at the back of the hall burst open, and out skipped Andrew's six-year-old sister, Bunty. She was dressed like a fairy in a white party frock and silver sandals, and had pink ribbons in her golden hair. The mystery of how big Andy could have a wee sister like Bunty was much discussed at Yett School.

'Hi, Chris!' squealed Bunty delightedly. 'I've been to Grandma's in Edinburgh. She bought me this new frock. Hi, Finn! Come and see my hamster!'

Finn said afterwards that he didn't stand a chance. Grabbing his hand with fingers like tiny tentacles and pulling like an Alsatian on a lead, Bunty yanked him out of the hall. For Chris, it was a nightmare moment. As soon as he saw Finn being pulled away he tried to run after him, but to his horror his way was blocked. As he stared into an expanse of red shirt he heard Andrew's voice, breathless with urgency, saying, 'No. Hang on a minute.'

Not for the first time, Chris thought he was going to wet himself with fear.

Later, he realized that it had been unlikely that Andrew would knee him in the groin there, in the hall of his own house, with his mother presumably within earshot. But at the time he was certain that he had been set up, that Bunty had been told to get Finn out of the way so that her brother could menace him. Chris pressed back against the banister, and with his usual self-contempt heard himself squeaking, 'If you hit me, Aldie, I'll –'

'I'm not going to hit you.' Andrew looked and sounded weary, but there was pleading in his voice as he went on urgently, 'Chris, listen. Don't be scared. I just want to speak to you alone for a minute.'

With his eye, Chris measured the distance to the door.

'I don't want —' he began, but Andrew interrupted.

'*Please*.' Before Chris could open his mouth again, he hurried on, 'Look. All I want is to tell you I'm sorry. I know I've been bad to you, but now I want to be friends. Please, won't you make up?'

It was the last speech Chris had ever expected to hear. He stared incredulously into the eyes that had always been so empty, but now seemed reflections of his own pain. It was almost worse than being attacked. And just for a moment, Chris wanted more than anything to believe Andrew, to say, 'Yes,' and let past hatred die. Only he couldn't. With despair he realized that he had suffered too much to let it be so easy. He couldn't stop hating, and he didn't trust Andrew's word. Vehemently he shook his head.

'No, I won't,' he said. He was going to add, 'You'd still beat me up on the Muirs bus, wouldn't you?' but changed his mind, saying instead, 'I could never be friends with someone whose dad is planning to ruin my dad's farm.'

He was disappointed to see relief in Andrew's eyes.

'Oh, I see,' said Andrew, as if the solution to a puzzle had suddenly dawned on him. 'Then if I —'

But he didn't have time to complete the sentence, because just then Finn reappeared. He was laughing and staggering, with Bunty riding high on his shoulders.

'Gee up, horse! Gee up!' she was screaming happily.

Andrew sighed and turned away from Chris. With unexpected gentleness, he took hold of Bunty and set her down on her feet.

'We're going to watch a film now,' he told her, making the choice himself. 'Come on. You can sit beside me.'

The rest of the afternoon passed, if not pleasantly, at least without any other ghastly incident. For an hour they watched a video film called *Fanfare for Mickey Mouse*, which Bunty at least found hilarious. While Finn and Chris lolled in armchairs like vast lemon sponge cakes, Bunty sat curled up close to Andrew on a sofa. She had a bag of jelly beans, and every time she put one into her own mouth, she popped one into his. Chris and Finn found this display of affection far more engrossing than the antics of Mickey Mouse.

Mrs Aldie had set out the birthday tea in the kitchen, a huge room with dark wooden cupboards, blue tiling and a magnificent view towards the mountains. She was casually kind, plying the boys with pizza and baked potatoes, and refilling their glasses with orange juice from time to time. If she noticed that Chris ate next to nothing she didn't comment, nor did she try, as Bess would have done, to ask jolly questions and make the party hum. Fortunately the boys' silence was covered by Bunty, who chattered and giggled happily, shared her juice with her teddy bear and helped Andrew to blow out the twelve candles on his birthday cake. Afterwards, one scrap of conversation stayed in Finn's mind.

'We're going to Portugal in the October holiday,' Bunty announced, 'to our other Pontevedra. Aren't we, Andrew?'

'Yeah,' Andrew agreed.

'We can't go in the summer 'cos of Daddy's families,' burbled on Bunty. 'Daddy's other families, you know. They go in the summer.'

'Eh?' said Finn.

He saw Mrs Aldie and Andrew catch each other's eye and laugh. It was the first time Andrew had looked amused; all afternoon he had been as white and strained as Chris. But it was Mrs Aldie who replied.

'I think I'd better explain,' she said. 'I don't want it to get about that Daddy has families dotted around the countryside – his reputation is bad enough as it is. The truth is,' she told Finn, 'that the minute my husband bought a villa in Portugal, he developed a bad conscience about it. He said it was wrong to leave it empty for weeks at a stretch when we couldn't be there. So he got in touch with a charity that provides holidays for families with sick children, and said they could use it.' She gave him a smile as she added, 'Of course, the way things have worked out, we're lucky if we can get a week there ourselves in the off-season.'

Against his will, Finn found himself liking her.

'Do you mind?' he asked.

'Not a bit,' she said, shaking her fair head.

Finn had been keeping what he hoped was a surreptitious eye on his watch. As soon as it was half-past six he said, 'I think we should push off now. I have to help my granny with the evening chores.'

Only Bunty expressed any regret. Mrs Aldie said, 'Just as you like,' while Andrew got up with alacrity to escort them to the front door. Bunty danced puppy-like at his heels.

'Goodbye,' she called. 'Come again soon.'

Chris shot out of the house and ran down the drive without looking back. Finn, who had had more than enough of his company in the last couple of days, let him go. Feeling that some small politeness was required, he asked Andrew, 'Will you be coming to the Roman field again?'

Andrew seemed hesitant.

'Well, not tomorrow, because Grandma's coming,' he said. 'Then on Monday we're going to Perth to the dentist. I'm not sure. Tuesday, maybe.' He paused, then asked, 'You haven't found anything yet, I take it?'

Finn shook his head. He was about to say goodbye when suddenly it occurred to him what Granny's first question was likely to be, when he got home.

'Oops! Hold on a minute,' he said, and ran back through the hall to the kitchen.

Mrs Aldie had started to clear the debris from the table and stack the plates in the dishwasher. She turned as Finn opened the door, and he was shocked to see how tired and unhappy she also looked.

'I – er, just came back to say thank you for having me,' he said.

For an uncomfortable moment Mrs Aldie's light brown eyes looked gravely into his. Then she said politely, 'You're welcome, Finn.'

Then Finn felt ashamed, and angry because he felt ashamed.

16 A Home Truth

That night Finn found it difficult to get to sleep. He did his best to make the dark hours pass by inventing a new episode of his waking dream; this time he was reducing Mr Curtis to jelly with pointed questions on his latest television programme, *The Finn Lochlan Interview*. But the make-believe of Mr Curtis's humiliation kept slipping away from him, and that was when Finn first realized that his new fantasy, like the old one about Hirsay, had ceased to interest him. It was being swept away by the stronger force of real events.

The real event which now refused to be banished from his mind was Andrew's birthday tea. As he tossed restlessly in the hot summer dark, Finn remembered painfully the miserable face of a boy hating every minute of his own birthday, and the hurt eyes of his mother as she discerned that the boys he had invited didn't want to be his friends. Finn blamed Granny, who had made him go to the Aldies' house against his better judgement, but he couldn't help recalling something she had said when he was arguing the toss with her on Thursday morning.

'Think shame of yourself, Finn. No human being is just a fat boy with smelly trainers. You'll learn to like him if you look for likeable things.'

Finn hadn't looked for likeable things, but he had seen them, just the same; Andrew being companionable with his little sister, his sharing of a joke with his mother, the improbable pleasantness of his face when he smiled. Damn, thought Finn, thumping the pillow with his fists. Why did I have to go to his house? It's making me soft about him. I knew I shouldn't have gone. The clock in the kitchen struck three before he fell asleep, wishing more than ever that Andrew would give him an excuse for returning to the uncomplicated dislike he used to feel.

At nine o'clock on Sunday morning, Bess rang up to say that Chris couldn't come over to play. He had been up half the night with a sore tummy, and was now asleep. Finn, who was more than half inclined to blame Chris for his own problem with Andrew, couldn't help feeling relieved. After breakfast he went out contentedly to help his father finish painting the window-sills. Sharing a tin of paint, they brushed in amicable silence for a while, then Finn said, 'Dad, listen. Is there any news about Mr Curtis's campaign? Has he actually done anything?'

He knew he was taking a risk, but this time Colin didn't lose his cool. He wiped a smear of paint off the window-frame with a rag, and gave one of his milder snorts.

'Once we'd calmed down,' he told Finn, 'Bess and Douglas and I decided that for the community's sake we should swallow our pride, and offer to help in any way we could. Douglas went over to Middle Corum to see Curtis yesterday, but didn't get over the doorstep. Curtis told him that he had his own method of dealing with Aldie – whatever that may mean – and shut the door in his face.'

'His own method? But what about the parish council?' frowned Finn, remembering Mr Curtis's words at the Jubilee Hall.

Colin made a rude noise.

'Curtis doesn't give a toss for the parish council,' he said sourly, 'for all his cant about democracy. He's an arrogant lout with land, money and power, and he does what he likes around here, if you ask me.'

'Then – does that mean he isn't organizing a campaign at all?' Finn wanted to know.

This time Colin's snort was a blast of disparagement.

'Organizing a campaign? Curtis couldn't organize two buns in a paper bag,' he said.

Finn thought this was funny, although he knew it was no laughing matter.

'So are you saying Mr Aldie will get his gravel pit permit – just like that?' he asked.

It seemed incredible, but Colin nodded gloomily.

'I don't see what's to stop him,' he said. 'A united community might have stood a chance, but the people round here seem to believe that Curtis can work miracles on his own. By the time they find out he can't, it will be too late. With so much unemployment in the area –'

He lifted his thin shoulders expressively.

'I see.' Finn was thoughtful as he removed a paint-brush hair from the wet paint with his fingernail. There was something he had wanted to ask for ages, but had been afraid of sounding defeatist. But now defeatism was in the air, so he took a deep breath and went ahead. 'And what about us, Dad? Will you and Douglas stay here with a gravel pit at the end of the road? Chris is talking about going back to Peru.'

The reply was forthright.

'Then he's a silly wee squirt, and you can tell him to forget it. Douglas and Bess and I have put everything we have into these farms. If – when – Aldie gets permission to start up his gravel pit, they won't be fit to live in and we won't be able to sell them. Your granny was right, Finn. We should have painted the house grey.'

Finn was shocked by this bitter speech, but he

learned something from it. No matter how hard his father and Douglas tried to believe that they put the community and the environment first, their real concern was to protect Frandy and Corumbeg. Just for a moment Finn was ready to condemn them as hypocrites, but then it occurred to him that really he was no better. All the time he had been lecturing Chris about the importance of finding a Roman fort, for the good of Glenaire, he had been spinning dreams of glory from which he had excluded Chris.

Finn dipped his brush in the paint and went on lightly stroking the kitchen window-sill. As he worked he thought over what his father had said, and soon decided that he felt the same way. It was natural to want to protect the home you loved, but the best way to do it was to band together in friendship with other people who felt as you did. If only the people at the Jubilee Hall had understood that, they would have stood a better chance of saving the glen, which was home to everyone. Now, since the notion that Mr Curtis could foil Mr Aldie alone was plainly moonshine, the only remaining hope surely was of proving that there had once been Romans in Glenaire. Not for the glory of Finn Lochlan. For the future of Corumbeg.

17 Sunday Afternoon

For lunch there was tomato soup, Finn's favourite. He was half-way through his second bowl when Granny, who was picking at bread and cheese, asked, 'Are you going over to see Chris this afternoon?'

Finn looked up uncertainly.

'I hadn't planned,' he said. 'If he's ill –'

He had supposed he was having a day off Chris, but when he saw his thoughts being read, he looked down at his bowl again. Granny, however, was not to be put off.

'He might still like to see you,' she persisted, and when Finn didn't answer, demanded plainly, 'Have you fallen out with him again?'

Finn felt his ears getting hot.

'Not exactly,' he muttered. 'It's just – well, he's so ruddy boring these days.'

He waited for a rebuke, not just for the swear-word. Granny was fond of Chris. So he was surprised when she nodded, thoughtfully pursing her lips.

'Yes,' she agreed. 'He's boring me too, with his pouting and flying into a rage every time he comes to a word he can't read. It really is a pity he has to start at another new school so soon.'

Finn raised his eyebrows.

'Do you think that's what's bugging him?' he said.

Chris had scarcely mentioned Muirs High School, and it had never crossed Finn's mind that he might be edgy about going there. Granny's tongue clicked impatiently.

'Heavens, yes,' she said. 'Of course it is. He's absolutely scared stiff.'

Colin always brought a book to the table, braving Granny's disapproval to avoid conversation. But now, probably because this was school talk, he joined in.

'It's not unusual,' he said. 'When I taught at Knightshill Academy there were always a few first-years snivelling into their hankies on their first day. They got over it. Is anyone else from Yett moving up to Muirs with Chris, Finn?'

'Andy Aldie,' Finn replied.

Colin guffawed.

'Then judging by his caterwauling at the Jubilee Hall, they'll be able to howl a duet,' he said hard-heartedly.

Finn couldn't help grinning at this, but Granny wasn't amused.

'Will they travel together?' she asked Finn, giving Colin a freezing look.

Finn laughed.

'Fat chance,' he said. 'Chris'll be going on the school bus, and Andy'll be going by Porsche.'

This was what he assumed. Andrew's father had to pass through Muirs on his way to work in Perth. Now it was Colin's turn to grin, but Granny ignored him.

'Are the Aldies very swanky?' she inquired.

'Not very,' said Finn. Then honesty forced him to add, 'Not at all, really.' It was true. The Aldies hadn't sent their children away to a posh school, like the Curtises, and Andrew never boasted about what he possessed. Finn was obliged to chalk up another likeable thing about him. 'Mr Aldie lends their villa in Portugal to families with sick kids,' he concluded, suddenly needing to be fair.

But Colin didn't want to hear likeable things about Mr Aldie. His good humour vanished and, whistling to Gruach, he left the kitchen with his book under his arm. It was Granny's face that assumed a gratified expression.

When he had done the washing up, Finn got out his bike and went the long way round to Frandy, enjoying the breeze in his hair and noticing how the rosehips were reddening, and the dusty hedgerows showing the first crackle of rust. Soon it would be time for school.

Chris was dressed and mooning about in the yard when Finn arrived. He was even paler than usual, and had raccoon-like dark patches around his eyes. But he said he was fine, and together he and Finn walked up on to the hill. When they got to the plank bridge over the Bindle burn they sat down, and let their legs dangle above the cold, greenish torrent. Its rapid tumbling sounded thunderous in the quiet afternoon. Chris was first to speak.

'I'm glad you came over,' he said. 'I want to apologize.'

'What for?'

'Being so bloody-minded and boring,' replied Chris. It sounded good, until he added slyly, 'It's no wonder you like big Andy better than me.'

The hint was so obvious that Finn felt a surge of annoyance. But because he was feeling more sympathetic than he had before lunch he stifled it, and tried to respond as Chris wanted him to.

'Don't be so daft. Of course I don't like big Andy better than you. We're mates, you and me. Always will be.'

Chris found this answer half-hearted, but didn't press the point.

'Well, thanks,' he muttered, turning his face away.

They sat in silence for a few minutes, spitting into the stream and watching the spittle being whirled away among the stones. Then Finn, thinking that it might help Chris to talk, said bluntly, 'Granny thinks you're in a panic about Muirs High. Are you?'

Chris leaned forward, staring down between his knees into the restless, weedy water. For a long, aching moment he longed to confide in Finn, and blurt out everything – how Andrew had menaced him all last term, how he had nightmares about the Muirs bus, about the dreadful moment when Andrew's apology had forced him to accept that he couldn't forget, forgive or trust. But he couldn't talk about it either, not to anyone. So at length he answered the original question, half truthfully.

'Yes, I am, I suppose. It's when I think of all the new subjects, and my reading still not being good enough.'

Finn made the same feebly encouraging remarks as everyone else.

'You'll be fine when you get there. I reckon everybody feels the same.'

They went back to the house and played a game of chess. Then they arranged to meet next day and Finn set off for home. As he pedalled along the main road he heard his name called, and saw Andrew and Bunty walking across the Roman field. They waved to him and he waved back, but didn't stop to talk. It was nearly five o'clock, and he had to see to the hens by himself because Sunday was Granny's half-day of rest.

18 The Head of Aurelian

Since the painting of Corumbeg was now all but finished, Finn and Chris were free to spend the whole of Monday at the Roman field. Bess, who was on holiday and desperate to do anything that might cheer Chris up, made a picnic lunch, and as the two boys ran down the hill they were more at ease with each other than they had been for a while. Even the limited confiding of Sunday afternoon had cleared the air. It was a sharp, slightly frosty morning, but the sun was burning back the early mist, heralding a fine day.

'We really must get a move on today,' remarked Finn, as they tramped across the dew-laden grass towards their excavation. 'Dad says Mr Curtis isn't doing a damn thing, and he reckons Mr Aldie's going to get his permit, no bother at all.'

'I know,' said Chris, as he hung the picnic bag on

a branch, out of the reach of peckish sheep. 'Dad says the same. He's still in a vile mood – says we're stuck here for ever, so I can shut my silly mouth about going back to Peru. Finn, do you think we really might find something Roman?'

Until now, his only reasons for wanting to dig had been to be with Finn, and to get Andrew into hot water with his father. But suddenly it seemed far more important to save Frandy, and get back the father he had known. Finn, newly realistic, shook his head.

'I don't know,' he said honestly. 'I just know we have to try.'

He had dreamed last night of a grey, desolate Corumbeg standing amid fields of ash. He couldn't shake off the dream.

The boys pulled out their spades and spread out the groundsheet to dry. Five of the marked squares had now been excavated to a depth of fifty centimetres, and the earth banked up along the side of the trench. Finn had no idea what a real excavation looked like, and would have been amazed to learn how professional his was. His finds were less so; a dreary assortment of tins, bottles and plastic cups had been stacked to await reburial. Finn, shaking his head ruefully, had remarked to Chris that perhaps in a hundred years a real archaeologist would rediscover them, and think he had been the first to discover that this was a twentieth-century picnic spot.

The boys now began patiently to turn over the sixth

square, but two broken saucers and a decomposing ram's horn were the only fruits of a morning's very hard work.

At midday they took their lunch down to the river, and spent an hour eating and laughing and splashing each other in the shallows. Andrew's name wasn't mentioned, and at one o'clock they went back to work. Finn, noticing that Chris still looked very pale, suggested that he should take it easy in the afternoon.

'If you take a trowel and sift over the earth we took out this morning, I'll start on the next square,' he said.

It was the next, but it was also the second-last square, and as he delved Finn really had to fight discouragement. He knew that if nothing was found they had wasted two whole weeks, and what then? His father reckoned that a Roman fort would have covered two hectares, and as Chris had said at the beginning, they couldn't dig up the whole field. His mind was full of anxious thoughts when suddenly he heard Chris hiss sharply through his teeth. He turned and saw that the white face had turned pink. Chris's grey eyes were wide with excitement.

'Finn,' he breathed. 'Come here. I think I've found something.'

Finn dropped his spade and cleared the trench in one bound.

'What is it?' he gasped, flopping down beside Chris in the earthy grass.

Together they stared at the palm of Chris's hand. On it lay two dull brown metal discs.

'Coins,' whispered Chris. 'They were there, at the bottom of the heap. They must have been in the first spadeful we took up.'

Finn tried to stay calm, but as he lifted one of the coins his fingers were shaking. He took it out from the shifting shadow of the trees into the sunlight, and Chris followed, the second coin squeezed tightly in his palm.

The one Finn had was rough and corroded at its edges, as if it had lain in the ground for a long time. But when he had gently rubbed away the earth, the impression was quite clear. Dry-mouthed, the boys stared at a bearded head with a garland of leaves, and round the edge the lettering, AURELIANUS: PIUS: IMP. On the other side was a picture of a Roman ship.

Finn gulped and said, 'Let's see the other one, Chris.'

The coin which Chris held had cleaned itself on the sweat of his hand. It was smaller than the first, but it too showed a garlanded head. On its reverse was the figure of a woman with wings and the word, IMPERATOR.

'We must take them to Dad,' said Finn. 'This is the first time I've been glad he was a Latin teacher.'

They had come on foot because the bike had a puncture, but Finn was sure they couldn't have got to Corumbeg faster if they'd had wings, like the woman on the coin. Leaving their spades in the grass, they ran along the road and up the long hill track, grunting with pain but buoyed up by triumph. Colin was in his vegetable garden, cutting cabbages for Perth market, when the two boys pounded through the yard.

'Dad! Come and see what we've found in the Roman field,' Finn was shrieking, and Colin, laughing at the two scarlet faces, put down his knife and came to the fence. When he saw what they were holding out, however, his amusement faded.

'What!' he exclaimed, pushing away Gruach, who thought that anything round and brown must be a chocolate drop.

'We – dug – them up,' puffed Chris, collapsing against the wire netting, while Finn supported himself on the gate.

Colin peered.

'Ye gods,' he said in his Latin-teachery way. 'But hang on, lads. I'll need my specs.'

Finn and Chris hopped up and down with impatience as he slowly pulled off his muddy boots at the back door. They followed him through the kitchen to his study across the hall, and hopped again while he found his spectacles and a magnifying glass. Colin studied the coins for a long time.

'Well?' ventured Finn, eventually.

But Colin wasn't going to be rushed. He looked at Finn over his glasses.

'How did you say you found these?' he asked provokingly, and Finn was obliged to waste time explaining about the excavation, and how Chris had turned up the coins in a pile of earth.

'You're trespassing,' Colin told him.

This was too much for Finn.

'Ach, to hell with trespassing, Dad,' he groaned. 'What about the coins?'

Colin grinned.

'Sorry,' he said. 'The coins. Well now. Of course, I'm not an expert, so I can't tell you whether these are genuine or not. If they're replicas, they're certainly very good ones –'

'Replicas?' squealed Chris indignantly. 'Why should they be replicas? We found them –'

'Yes, I know. But hang on a minute, Chris. There's a problem.'

It took time for these dire words to sink in. Then Finn asked in a tight, wary voice, 'What kind of problem?'

Colin scratched his nose.

'Well, it's this guy Aurelian,' he said. 'He was a Roman emperor, right enough. These letters round the head stand for, "Aurelian, the dutiful emperor". The word "imperator" on the other coin means "emperor" in Latin.'

'So?' prompted Chris nervously.

Colin shook his head.

'The snag is that Aurelian was emperor late in the third century A D. That was nearly two hundred years after the Romans withdrew south, and the forts around here were abandoned. Whoever dropped these coins in your wee excavation, boys, it certainly wasn't a Roman.' Colin looked at their stricken faces, then said more gently than usual, 'I think maybe somebody's been having you on.'

Finn and Chris looked at each other, haggard with disappointment and disbelief.

'But who?' cried Chris. 'Who even knew we were there?'

Put like that, of course, the answer was obvious, and they said it together.

'Big Andy.'

19 A Nasty Plan

The boys left Colin trying to decipher the lettering on the head of the second coin, and went upstairs to Finn's room. Already their feelings of shock and chagrin were changing to an angry desire for revenge.

'It isn't as if there's any doubt about it,' said Chris grimly, as he bounced himself on to the end of Finn's bed. 'Remember when Mrs Ritchie brought those aerial photographs of the Roman camp at Inchtuthil to show us? Big Andy turned up next day with some Roman coins. Said his dad had bought them on a business trip to Turkey, I think it was. They must be the same ones.'

'Yes,' agreed Finn. 'And he was in the Roman field with wee Bunty yesterday. I saw them on my way back from your place. He must've been planting them, the dirty rat.' He stared out of the window with hard eyes, feeling angry and foolish, yet bewildered too. 'I can't understand it,' he said. 'He was so pleased when I said he could help, and you have to admit he hasn't put a foot wrong since the day he brought back your pencil case. He even invited us to his birthday tea, for God's sake. And now this.'

He had longed for an excuse to hate Andrew again, but now that he had it, he found it wasn't what he wanted at all. The likeable things had been mounting up, and he felt as hurt as if he had been betrayed by a friend. Chris's reaction was predictable.

'People like him never change,' he said, and couldn't smother a glow of triumph because now Finn would have to accept that this was true. But when he was tempted to add sniffily, 'And he had the cheek on Saturday to ask me to be friends,' something stopped him. Instead he said in a hard, vindictive voice, 'He'll have to be punished.'

'Yes,' agreed Finn. 'He deserves it. Only, how?'

'A booby-trap,' suggested Chris. 'Down at the Roman field. Something that'll get him dirty and make him look silly, but not hurt him because then we'd get into big trouble.'

The thought of the big trouble he would get into on the Muirs bus, if the booby-trap worked, didn't even occur to him. The thirst for revenge was making him reckless, as well as cruel.

Finn thought for a moment, then he nodded.

'I know,' he said. 'We can fix something on a tree, like when you put a pail of water on top of a door, and it falls down when someone opens it.'

'How do we make it fall?' asked Chris, with a faint, anticipatory grin.

'Easy,' said Finn. 'We fill a plastic bucket with water and tie a long thread to the handle. We put the bucket up in the fork of a tree and let the thread hang down. One of us holds the end while the other gets him to look at something underneath, then hey, presto! If the bucket's properly balanced, one tweak of the thread will bring the water down on top of him.'

Chris sniggered.

'Great,' he enthused. 'We'll have to be ready to sprint, though.'

'He'll be in no state to,' said Finn callously.

When they went back to the Roman field to tidy away the tools they had abandoned earlier, Finn and Chris took with them a green plastic bucket and a reel of strong black thread from Granny's sewing basket. Down on the river bank they filled the bucket with water and mixed in a few trowelfuls of gritty brown mud. Conveniently there was an oak with low branches and plenty of leaves, just over the place where Chris had found the coins. Finn climbed on to the lowest bough, and when Chris passed the bucket up to him, managed to balance it where it was lightly supported by leafy twigs. He tied the end of the thread to the handle and let down the reel; when it reached ground level Chris broke it off and anchored the other end with a stone.

'I'll say, "Oh, look, Andy! I think I've found a Roman coin,"' he said with bitter relish. 'Then when he comes over I'll skip out of the way, and –'

'Splat,' said Finn, jumping lightly down. But then he frowned, and looked up anxiously at the precariously balanced bucket. 'There's only one thing,' he added.

'What?'

'I think we should try to lure Andy here tonight. On the farming forecast this morning it said that the wind would rise after dark. If that happens, the bucket will capsize before we get here tomorrow.'

'Hm,' said Chris doubtfully. 'Won't he smell a rat?'

Finn snorted.

'No way,' he said. 'Not if we tell him we're dying to share something exciting we've found. I know. I'll ring him up while Granny's out at the hens. I'll be all mysterious, and ask him to meet us here at half-past seven. After supper, you say you're nipping over to my place for an hour, and I'll say I'm nipping over to your place for an hour. I'll meet you at the log bridge in Fear Wood at – say, seven-fifteen, then we can run down the forestry track to the main road. Nobody at home will see us, and if the Aldies kick up a stink about Andy getting soaked, we can swear we were playing in the wood all the time.'

Finn wasn't normally a cruel person, and usually

118

he didn't tell lies. But his anger at the trick Andrew had played on him with the coins was made even more bitter by a feeling that he had been made a fool of in a more important way. He had only realized that he now liked Andrew in the same moment when he found himself betrayed.

It was Mrs Aldie who answered the telephone.

'Muirs five-two-eight-two-three. Who's speaking, please?'

Finn, knowing that Granny was in the henhouse and his father among the vegetables, didn't even have to lower his voice.

'Mrs Aldie? It's Finn Lochlan. Can I speak to Andrew, please?'

'Oh.' There was a brief pause. Presumably Andrew's phone calls were few and far between. Then Mrs Aldie said, 'Of course, Finn. Hold on. I think he's in the sitting-room.'

She sounded pleased, but Finn wasn't in the mood to feel bad about her either. He heard her putting down the receiver, then the sound of Australian voices shouting on the Aldies' television. Andrew came on the line.

'What do you want?' he asked cautiously.

Finn had his speech ready.

'Hey, Andy, listen,' he said, infusing his voice with false warmth. 'You'll never believe this, but we've found something in the Roman field. I wanted to tell you before we tell anyone else – seeing you helped us, and didn't tell your dad what we were doing.'

He didn't include Chris in this expression of good-heartedness; that would stretch Andrew's credulity too far.

'I see. What did you find?' asked Andrew, sounding so innocent that Finn shook his fist at the telephone.

But he managed to go on in the same friendly tone.

'No – no. I won't tell you now. I want it to be a surprise,' he said. 'Can you come over to the Roman field at half-past seven? Chris and I are so excited, we thought we'd work on a bit after supper, just in case there are – well, some more of what we've found.'

He was sure he would never fall for such a story, and had an anxious moment before Andrew said, 'Yeah. OK. See you, then.'

'Speak to you later,' said Finn, and put the phone down.

What a prize fool, he thought contemptuously.

20 A Tale Underground

The sheep were to blame, if you can blame sheep for anything. When Chris and Finn came down the forestry track at half-past seven, Andrew was lounging against the gate of the Roman field. He had reassumed his blank expression, and after the briefest of greetings they climbed over and set out across the grass. They walked in single file, with Finn leading, then Andrew with Chris close on his heels – too close, as it turned out. They were half-way across when they noticed that Mr Aldie's sheep were having a meeting; the whole flock was huddled in a woolly white mass in front of the oak wood, blocking the boys' usual access to their excavation.

Without looking back, Finn began to make a detour

to his left. He had gone only a few metres when he heard Andrew say, 'Ow!' and Chris emit a squawk of alarm. When he turned round, both his companions had disappeared.

It had happened in an instant. Andrew said afterwards that it was his fault for being so heavy, which was nonsense, but certainly his weight did break the rotting, grass-covered wooden disc which a moment earlier had supported Finn. Chris saw him vanish into the ground and tried to pull up, but too late. His boot slipped, and he went feet first into the hole which Andrew's fall had opened. By a miracle he didn't fall on Andrew and break his neck, but made a soft landing beside him in thick mud. It seemed pitch dark after the daylight, but Chris could hear Andrew's breathing, and panic grabbed his throat.

'Finn!' he screamed. 'Help! Finn!'

Finn, who had been too astounded to move, was jolted into action by the subterranean howls. He began to run, then stopped abruptly. If Andrew and Chris had fallen down a hole, he thought, he must be careful not to do the same. Testing the ground carefully with his toe, he crept nervously back along the line he thought he had taken.

'It's all right, Chris. I'm coming,' he shouted, in answer to the ever more desperate cries.

Only it wasn't all right. Finn arrived suddenly at a gaping hole in the turf, with broken wood and torn tussocks hanging loosely around its rim. Lying down on his front, he edged forward and stuck out his head, wrinkling his nose at the horrible, stagnant smell. About three metres down he could see the two boys, but knew he couldn't possibly reach them.

'Chris!' he called. 'Andy! Are you hurt?'

Chris was making incoherent, snivelling noises, but Andrew replied calmly, his voice echoing in the shaft.

'Finn! I'm not hurt, and I don't think Chris is. We're in some kind of well. It has brick walls, but there's no water in it, only mud. Can you go for help?'

'Sure,' called back Finn, relieved. 'I'll run to your house. It's nearest.'

'No, don't,' answered the echoing voice. 'Sorry — there's no one in. Dad's at the youth club he runs in Perth, and Mum's taken Bunty to the carnival on Muirs Green.'

Finn groaned.

'And this is my dad's night out at Muirs Bridge Club,' he said. 'I'll have to go to Frandy. Chris, is Douglas at home?'

'Yes,' wailed Chris. 'But Finn, don't leave me.'

This was one of many occasions recently when Finn would have enjoyed kicking Chris's behind.

'Don't be such an ass,' he snapped. 'Andy, listen. It isn't much further to Frandy than it is to my place. I'll be back as soon as I can.'

'Cheers, Finn. Sorry about this,' Andrew replied.

Through a blur of fear, Chris saw Finn withdraw his head from the ragged circle of light at the mouth of the well. He felt abandoned and absolutely terrified.

'My dad's coming,' he warned Andrew. 'If you hit me –'

'Oh, God.' Andrew sounded as if he couldn't believe this was happening again. 'How often do I have to say it? I'm not going to hit you. Now why don't we sit down, nice and quiet, and wait for your dad to come? There's a little ledge,' he added, sliding his bottom down the brick wall towards the floor.

Somehow it got through to Chris that he wasn't immediately threatened. Pulling himself together, he too found the ledge which stuck out from the wall. He sat down, drawing up his knees to avoid touching Andrew in the narrow space. Now that his eyes had become accustomed to the faint light, he could see the other boy looking tired and grey. There was silence for a while, then Andrew said, 'Chris –'

'I don't want to talk.'

Andrew shrugged.

'OK. You don't have to,' he said. 'But I want to talk, and you'll just have to listen, won't you?' Chris didn't say yes, but he couldn't say no, and after a pause Andrew went on. 'I know you don't want to be friends with me, and I don't much care any more whether I'm friends with you. I should have known better, and I'm sorry I bothered you. But just for the record – it was the psychologist's idea, not mine. He had the mad idea that if I was nice to you, you would be nice to me.'

'Psychologist?' Chris couldn't help saying curiously. 'What psychologist?'

He heard Andrew sigh.

'Before the summer holidays,' he said, 'Mrs Ritchie came to see my mum and dad. She told them my behaviour was so bad that before I started at a new school I should see a child psychologist. She thought that if he could find out why I knocked other kids about, maybe he could help me to stop. So I was dragged off to a guy in Perth with funny specs and a beard like Santa Claus. At first I thought he was just a joke, but I got to like him. He really cared about me.'

Shocked but fascinated, Chris was drawn into conversation against his will.

'And did he find out why you knocked other kids about?' he asked.

Andrew laughed shortly.

'I didn't need a psychologist to tell me that,' he said. He paused, then went on again, 'When I was wee, I was dying to go to school. We had a calendar in the kitchen, and every morning for about a year I crossed off the date. When I got new trousers and a sweatshirt with "Yett School" on the front, it was the best day of my life.'

'And?' prompted Chris.

'On my first day in Primary One, a boy called Angus Danby came up to me in the playground and called me a fat pig. I must've been really stupid, because it was the first time I realized I was fat.' Andrew frowned, reliving a terrible moment, then he continued. 'Danby shouted, "See this fat pig!" and a lot of other kids came running over. They made a circle round me and started chanting, "Fat pig! Fat pig!" When I tried to break out of the circle they wouldn't let me, so I headbutted Angus Danby, and he went howling to Miss Barry. She said I was a wicked little boy, and made me stand with my face to the wall. I suppose I should have got over it, but I reckon finding out that I was fat and wicked in one morning was too much for me. Nobody's ever liked me and – oh God, I hated Yett School.'

Chris's acute discomfort had little to do with being covered with mud at the bottom of a well.

'That was rotten,' he said, meaning it. But then, 'All the same – why did you have to pick on me?'

'I don't know,' replied Andrew candidly. 'I got that I just couldn't help it. But Dr Mearns – he's the psychologist – said that I could, if I wanted to. He said that twelve-year-olds aren't as savage as young kids, and I should try to forget what happened seven years ago. He said that a new school was a new beginning, and that if I was friendly and kept my mitts off people, they wouldn't mind me being fat and having hair like candy floss.' If he noticed Chris squirming with embarrassment he didn't comment, but went on with a shake of his head, 'Some hope! I'm scared stiff about going to Muirs High, and Mum and Dad thought that if I tried to make friends with you, it would be easier for me. The day I picked up your pencil case in Fear Wood, I was on my way to your place to ask you to come to tea.'

'But you didn't.'

Andrew smiled grimly.

'No. When I saw you quaking like a jelly and nearly wetting your pants, I decided it wasn't the right time.'

Chris, remembering the occasion well, let this pass.

'But you still said, "See you at the bus stop,"' he pointed out, and heard Andrew make an exasperated sound.

'I know. It was out before I thought,' he replied. 'I was kicking myself all the way down the road.'

There was silence at the bottom of the well. In the fading circle of sky overhead, two stars began to shine.

Eventually Chris said, 'Look –' but Andrew wasn't finished yet.

'I'm sorry about the Roman coins,' he said.

'Oh, hell,' muttered Chris.

'I didn't do it to play a trick on you, I swear it,' said Andrew earnestly. 'Dr Mearns kept telling me what a lot I was missing by not having friends, and I was desperate to make it with you and Finn – you particularly, because we're both going to Muirs High. When Finn said I could help in the Roman field I thought I was getting somewhere, but I soon saw you didn't want to know me. Then I started wondering if it was because of Dad's gravel pit – because your dad was so against it. I wanted to show you I was really against it too. That was why I nagged Mum into taking me to the meeting, so that I could sign the protest letter. Only she had other ideas about that.'

Chris opened his mouth to say something like, 'Well, you did try,' but Andrew just went on with his story.

'When you said at my birthday tea that you wouldn't be friends with me because my dad wanted to ruin your dad's farm, I was sure I was right. I tried to persuade Dad to stop, but he said sorry, there were principles at stake. That was when I got the idea of planting the coins. I was sure Dad had forgotten we had them, and I reckoned that if you found them, your dad and Mr Lochlan might be able to stop Dad getting a permit. Then you might be friends with me.'

Chris was mortified. Thank God he doesn't know about the booby-trap, he thought.

'They were the wrong date,' he explained. 'Finn's dad knew. But how did you know we'd rumbled you?'

'When Finn rang up,' was the amused reply. 'He was so ruddy matey. I'm not that stupid. Your bucket's in our garage, by the way.'

Chris tried feebly to brazen it out.

'What bucket?' he asked.

'You know fine,' said Andrew, on the verge of laughter. 'I went over after tea to find out what little treat you'd set up for me.' Then the laughter escaped. 'Not really worth the trouble,' he chuckled. 'By the time I got there the bucket had fallen down. I just came tonight to see your faces.'

Chris could feel his cheeks burning, in contrast to the rest of him, which was icy cold.

'Look –' he began again, but once more Andrew interrupted him.

'It's OK,' he said. 'From your point of view, I deserved it. No hard feelings.' And as the distant drone of a motor engine rose to a roar as Douglas drove the pick-up over the grass, he got to his feet and looked down at Chris through the gloom. 'Anyway,' he concluded, 'you're shot of me now. Just try to stop looking like a scared rabbit every time you see me. I've never hit you, and I never shall.'

Before Chris could think of an answer, headlights beamed across the mouth of the well. He heard his father's voice. Rescue had come.

21 Samian Ware

Finn, having been sharply ticked off for going AWOL by Douglas, his father and Granny, went to bed and slept soundly through the windy night. In the morning, however, he got up feeling depressed and ashamed. As he went about his chores in the cold morning light he regretted many things, but most of all his behaviour the previous day. Whatever had prompted Andrew to plant the coins in the Roman field, he had been brave and grown-up last night, and Finn was still reeling from the shock of Chris's remark in the back of the pick-up on the way home.

'He was really nice, and I wish I hadn't been so rotten to him.'

The only consolation, Finn thought, was that Andrew didn't know about the booby-trap. If he had known that his plastic bucket was in the Aldies' garage, his cup of shame would have been full to the brim. As he ate his breakfast he began to dread meeting Chris, and the prospect of a long morning discussing Andrew. Chris's arrival, however, was so dramatic that yesterday's events suddenly stopped being so interesting.

At ten to nine, when Granny was hoovering the hall and Finn was drying the breakfast dishes, Douglas's pick-up came bouncing up the hill and screeched to a halt outside the back door. The kitchen door flew open and Douglas strode in, with Chris dancing excitedly at his heels. He seemed to have made a remarkable recovery from his fright in the well.

'Colin,' commanded Douglas. 'Put on your specs, and come and look at this.'

'I'll fetch Granny Lochlan,' said Chris, and hurried into the hall.

The wailing of the Hoover ceased, and a moment later they were all round the kitchen table. Douglas took from his pocket what looked like a broken piece of terracotta flowerpot, roughly six centimetres square, and laid it gently on the blue tablecloth.

Finn leaned over and looked at it closely. He saw that the surface was shiny, and embossed with a design that looked like leaves. It meant nothing to him until he glanced up at his father's face. Colin's mouth was a whistling "O" of astonishment, and his eyes were also round behind his glasses.

'Ye gods!' he exclaimed. 'Where on earth did you find this?'

He lifted the object reverently and carried it to the window. While he stood examining it, Douglas explained.

'I found it on the floor of the pick-up this morning. It must have been sticking to Chris's boot when I hauled him out of the well. Is it what I think it is, Colin?'

It was typical of Colin, Finn thought with amusement, that even at a moment like this he delivered a little teachery lecture.

'It's impossible for me to say with certainty, of course. However, the colour, gloss and what I can see of the design are typical of a kind of Roman pottery called Samian ware. It was common all over the Empire, and a lot of it has been unearthed in Scotland. It's of Agricola's period.'

As always at a time of crisis, Granny got up and put on the kettle. Chris helped her to spoon coffee into mugs while Finn pored over the ordinary-looking piece of pottery, too amazed and delighted to speak. For the first and only time he imagined the Romans as living beings, like himself. In his mind's eye he saw the wooden fort beside the Aire, and the columns of armoured men marching behind their eagle standards. He saw the bright plumes of the cavalry, and heard the braying of trumpets in the cold morning mist. He touched the terracotta shard with his finger and thought, Romans touched this too. At one time he would have been wild with jealousy because he hadn't found it, but now that didn't seem to matter at all.

Douglas was saying to Colin, 'I arranged with Bess that if you thought it was Roman, I'd give her a ring at the lab. She'll go over to the museum at lunchtime, and try to make an appointment for us to see the curator tomorrow. She says he's directed other excavations around here, so he'll know how to proceed. This could be the saving of us, Colin.'

'Aye, so it maybe could,' agreed Colin emotionally, and less grammatically than usual.

Chris, carrying mugs of coffee, said he didn't think he could wait until tomorrow.

'Couldn't Mum make an appointment for us to go today?' he asked plaintively.

'Us?' teased Douglas, taking his mug. 'You thinking of coming, are you?'

Chris's eyes popped indignantly.

'Of course we're coming,' he exploded. 'We've been digging up that stupid field for weeks, and I found the Roman whatsit, didn't I?' He handed a mug to Colin, then added, laughing, 'Well, maybe not. Maybe big Andy found it. At least he opened up the hole.'

Finn giggled, but Douglas groaned.

'Big Andy,' he repeated. 'Lord, that kid was some weight. When he came up on the rope, it was like meeting myself at the same age.'

This remark made Chris and Finn glance at each

133

other shamefacedly, but nothing could really dampen their spirits. After a long bath, Chris had slept like a top, and in the morning had known what he must say to Andrew. In spite of everything, he was feeling better than he had for months.

When they had drunk their coffee, the boys left the house and went up on to the hill. It was a bright day, with racing clouds and curlews fluting above the opening heather. Finn and Chris followed the Bindle burn until they came once more to the plank bridge where they had sat on Sunday afternoon.

'Only two days ago,' said Chris, as he sat down and swung his legs over the edge. 'It seems ages to me.'

'A lot's happened,' said Finn.

Then Chris told Finn everything, from Andrew's bullying at school last term to last night's story in the well. He spared no detail discreditable to himself, and even when Finn said, 'Don't blame yourself. If I'd known his mum and dad were sending him on the bus, I'd have been worried for you,' he didn't feel glad of the excuse.

'He said he was sorry and asked me to be friends at his birthday tea,' he confessed, 'and I behaved like a stupid squit. And I was the one who put it around that he had smelly trainers, actually,' he concluded sheepishly.

'Had he?' asked Finn, unable to prevent his lips twitching.

'I don't know. I never smelt them,' replied Chris, and they laughed because they couldn't help it. But then Chris shook his head and went on, 'If only I'd known that he was scared of going to Muirs High too! What a mean pig I've been.'

Finn also shook his head.

'If you have,' he said, 'I've been a worse one. First I bullied you into helping me in the Roman field, then I forced you to let Andy join in, even though I knew you hated the idea. And I called him an outsider, and used him, just like I was using you.' He spat into the Bindle, wondering whether to tell all, then decided that since Chris had told everything, so must he. 'I wanted to get my name in the paper,' he admitted. '"Young archaeologist finds Roman treasure", you know. "Wonder boy saves Glenaire".'

Chris gave him an amused, sidelong look.

'Help me! Finn's Roman fort,' he said. 'I thought you stopped playing games like that when you fell down the cliff on Hirsay.'

'I have now,' Finn vowed.

'Till next time,' grinned Chris.

'Let's take our rods down to Andy's place and ask him if he wants to go fishing,' suggested Finn, and Chris agreed.

But when they got to La Pontevedra there was no one at home. In the afternoon there was still no one at home, and when Chris rang up at half-past six there was no reply.

'He's probably gone to Edinburgh again,' said Finn. 'Never mind. We can see him tomorrow, as soon as we get back.'

22 At the Museum

Because Bess had to leave for work at half-past seven, and the appointment she had made with Dr Price wasn't until eleven, Finn and Chris travelled to Glasgow in the back of the Corumbeg Land Rover. While their fathers sat in front discussing sheep, the two boys lolled on the back seat. Too happy to chatter, they gazed out of the window as green fields dropped back along the motorway, merging at last into the dusty stone and concrete sprawl of the city suburbs.

'I wouldn't fancy living here now, would you?' asked Finn, eyeing critically the dirty pavements and rows of uniform houses.

'No way,' agreed Chris, who for many months had longed to live anywhere that wasn't Frandy Farm. 'Glenaire's our place now, and it's going to be great, once this gravel pit business is blown out of the water.'

To Chris and Finn, the visit to the museum was only a formality. The only diggers they anticipated in the Roman field now were archaeologists with spades.

'Mr Aldie will be livid, I suppose,' said Finn, 'but Andy will be pleased.'

The museum was an ornate nineteenth-century building, across a narrow street from the glass and concrete tower block where Bess had her laboratory. Colin was lucky, finding a parking space outside. Feeling important, the boys followed Douglas and Colin through heavy swing doors into a gloomy, marble-floored hall. With its pointed Gothic windows it was like a church, and had the same reverent, hushed atmosphere. The boys giggled at the echo of their own footsteps, and fully expected the woman behind the reception desk to frown over her glasses and say, 'Sh-sh-sh!'

Instead she took Colin's name, smiled and spoke on a telephone.

'Dr Price will see you straight away,' she said.

The four from Glenaire followed her down a long corridor with glass display cases on either side; Finn and Chris glimpsed pieces of pottery similar to their own, and nudged each other in satisfaction. At the end of the corridor was Dr Price's office. The receptionist showed them in.

The director of the museum was a small, bearded man in a striped suit and a club tie. He had a deadpan face and a dry manner, but he shook hands civilly and found chairs for them all. It had been decided that Colin would tell the story and Finn thought he did it well, explaining clearly how and where the shard of pottery had been found.

'The well itself isn't Roman,' said Colin, who had done his homework at Muirs Public Library yesterday. 'It's all that's left of an eighteenth-century brewery. But if the shard is Samian ware, there's likely to be a lot more, isn't there?'

Dr Price lifted the terracotta fragment and held it between white fingertips. He showed none of the excitement and astonishment which the boys had anticipated, and it went through Finn's mind that he was a boring old stick. But he reminded himself that Dr Price had seen a lot of Roman remains in his time, which no doubt accounted for his cool. At length the director laid their find on the desk in front of him and nodded his balding head.

'Yes,' he said. 'I can have it tested for you, of course, but I'd say it's almost certainly Samian pottery from the first century A.D.'

'So it does mean there was a Roman fort in Glenaire in Agricola's time, doesn't it?' burst out Finn, unable to hold back any longer.

Dr Price smiled frostily.

'It would be an indication,' he said, 'though not sufficient proof in itself.'

Finn and Chris just managed not to groan out loud. Douglas gave them a slight, warning shake of his head, then spoke to Dr Price. There was nothing in his calm, even voice to suggest how desperately Dr Price's response mattered to them all.

'What we need to know,' he said, 'is whether you think an excavation is warranted. The owner of the field where this shard came from is planning to turn it into a gravel pit. If he's to be stopped, we must move quickly.'

All four of them stared at the director, holding their breath as they waited for his reply. Minutes seemed to pass, and Chris thought he was going to scream. Then Dr Price shook his head, and all the optimism of the last twenty-four hours dispersed like a sigh.

'The field may indeed be the site of a Roman fort,' he said, not unkindly, for he saw their disappointment, 'although nowadays that wouldn't necessarily prevent its becoming a gravel pit. At best it would delay it – if we could afford an excavation, which we can't. All museums are strapped for cash these days, and we couldn't justify the expense of a dig which would only turn up more of what we have already. Your find will be recorded, of course, but – well, I'm sorry. This just isn't the right time.'

'So that's that,' said Finn bleakly, as they came out of the tranquil museum into the busy street.

They had arranged to meet Bess for lunch, expecting it to be a celebration. In fact, it was just a waste of money. They went to an Indian restaurant which had been the Coopers' favourite when they lived in Glasgow, but even Chris and Finn were too choked to enjoy the meal. This snuffing out of their last hope of beating Mr Aldie seemed worse than if Chris hadn't picked up the piece of Samian ware at all.

The journey home was long and silent, the grey, autumnal afternoon a suitable setting for sad, private thoughts. No one could have imagined that for them all the worst shock of the day was still to come, but so it proved. As the Land Rover approached the turn-off to Frandy, Colin roused himself and said hospitably to Douglas, 'Come home with us, and have a cup of tea with Granny. She usually bakes on Wednesdays, doesn't she, Finn?'

'Cheese scones today,' shuddered Finn, whose prawn korma was still heavy in his stomach.

But Douglas said, 'Thanks. We'd like that, wouldn't we, Chris?' and Chris, who knew that since the well episode his father had been trying to rebuild their old comradeship, said, 'Sure, Dad. We're in no hurry.'

He had come close to hating Douglas in the past few weeks, but he felt no resentment now. He had been forced to work things out for himself, and although it had been hard, he was glad. Once he had made his peace with Andrew, Chris thought he could even look forward to Muirs High School.

So Colin drove on to Corumbeg, where they all got out of the Land Rover and piled into the kitchen. They thought they were the only ones with a sad story to tell, but when they saw the expression on Granny's thin old face, words failed on their lips.

23 Thugs

Granny had lit the fire, and she was sitting over it with her arms crossed over her chest. She looked as if she felt very cold, and couldn't get herself warm. It was plain that she had had some terrible shock, and when she got to her feet Colin, very unusually, went to support her.

'What's the matter, Mother?' he asked anxiously. 'Are you ill?'

Granny blinked and shook her head.

'No,' she said huskily. 'But something terrible has happened, and I can't take it in. Just after you left this morning, the postman came. He told me that Mr Aldie's boy – Andrew, isn't it? – was set on last night by two thugs, and beaten half to death. Oh, Colin! Who would do such a thing? Aren't children safe anywhere?'

Chris gasped and went as white as a sheet, but Finn understood why Granny was so upset. Of course she was sorry for Andrew, but she didn't know him. All day she had been shuddering because the victim might have been Finn. She had thought he was safe in Glenaire. Now she knew he wasn't. Normally Finn was as undemonstrative as his father, but now he strode over to Granny and gave her a hug. He felt her fingers stroking his head, but then she gently disengaged his arms and returned to her chair.

'I'm sorry,' she said, adding fretfully, 'Weakness. Old age.'

It was Douglas who boiled the kettle and tossed teabags into five mugs. He brought some tea to Granny, and when she had sipped a little she was able to tell them the rest of the postman's story.

'Mrs Aldie and the children had been to Strathyre for the day. They got back about half-past eight, and she went upstairs to put the little one to bed. She thinks that the boy must have had the idea of walking towards the village to meet his father, who was due back from Perth about nine, but he didn't tell her he was going out. The first she knew was when Mrs Clark from the post office came knocking at the door. The Clarks had been out walking their dogs, and found Andrew lying by the roadside between Yett and Middle Corum. Mr Clark called an ambulance, and he was rushed to Perth Infirmary.'

'Is Andrew badly hurt?' asked Chris, remembering

bleakly that he had parted from Andrew on Monday night without a friendly word.

He had thought there was plenty of time. Granny heard the distress in his voice, and answered as comfortingly as she could.

'He's badly hurt, yes,' she said, 'but he isn't going to die. The postman says he has severe concussion and broken ribs, and bruising all over his body.'

Finn and Chris imagined the attack and winced, while Douglas asked harshly, 'Do the police have any idea who did it?'

Granny shook her head.

'I couldn't say, Douglas,' she replied. Finn saw her shiver. 'The postman says this sort of thing happens in the country more often than you'd think,' she sighed.

'It's called mindless violence,' said Finn angrily, but Douglas and Colin exchanged sceptical looks.

'I'll be surprised if there isn't a mind behind this violence,' said Douglas grimly.

The rest of the week passed leadenly. On Thursday, Granny spent the day in bed, less because she was ill than because she was too miserable to get up. After he had taken her some tea and the newspaper, Finn went over to Frandy. In a thin smirr of rain he and Chris went down to the Roman field, to put back the turf on their excavation and fetch up their tools. It was hard work, but it gave them something to do, and their sadness at this unhappy ending was blunted by their greater sorrow for Andrew.

'If only I'd said something nice to him before I got into the pick-up,' said Chris, blaming himself.

'You weren't to know,' Finn replied.

As they crossed the field for the last time, they met a tractor, with a trailer full of earth and stones. Mr Aldie had sent workmen to fill in the well. Finn felt as if the door to a treasure cave was being closed for ever, but it scarcely seemed to matter any more.

On Friday, Douglas took the two boys to Perth to collect the rest of Chris's school uniform and spend an hour at the swimming pool, but no one enjoyed the outing. In the evening, Bess telephoned Mrs Aldie to ask how Andrew was, and learned that he was still in hospital. Mrs Aldie said that he was making progress, but was suffering from a bad headache and double vision. Her voice was very calm, which meant, according to Bess, that she was rapidly coming to the end of her tether.

On Saturday morning Douglas went down to Yett post office to buy stamps. He came back with a piece of news which didn't surprise him, or Colin, but shocked everyone else rigid. It seemed that Andrew had recovered sufficiently to describe his attackers, and had given the police the lead they were looking for. The previous afternoon a police car had arrived at Middle Corum, and shortly afterwards Mr Curtis's two teenage sons had been taken away to Muirs police station for questioning. In the evening they were charged with assaulting Andrew, and the police started questioning their father.

'So now we know what Curtis meant when he told me he had his own method of dealing with Aldie,' said Douglas, in deep disgust. 'A savage wouldn't stoop so low.' It was small comfort to learn also that Mr Curtis's popularity was now non-existent. 'Of all the rabble who cheered him at the Jubilee Hall,' Douglas said, 'not half a dozen would support him now.'

24 Mr Aldie

Bess had invited the Lochlans to supper on Saturday,
but Granny had a headache, so they came on Sunday
instead. Douglas opened a bottle of wine, and when
the two families were seated round the kitchen table
eating chicken casserole, it seemed superficially that
nothing had changed at all.

At a deeper level, however, they all felt that nothing
would ever be the same again, and that new realities
had to be faced. The nightmare of the gravel pit would
come true, and the parents who had brought their
children to the country to avoid the dangers of city life
would no longer be so confident about their safety.
They also had to face the fact that a near neighbour, a
man with whom Colin had once been on quite friendly
terms, was a ruffian without a care for human life, as

long as he could keep Glenaire the way he wanted it to be.

Still, that evening there was the kind of peace that comes when the worst has happened, and been accepted. Douglas and Colin agreed that they would have to abandon growing vegetables, but there was also talk of buying more sheep and moving them further up the hill, where the wind-blown dust wouldn't reach them. Bess had heard of someone who was likely to give them a keen price for double-glazing, which she assured Granny would keep the gravel dust out of the house.

'We had it in Glasgow,' she said, 'and it really did shut out noise and dirt. We lived on a very busy road.'

They had eaten their lemon pudding, and it was almost dark when Douglas got up to make the coffee. In a lull in the conversation they were surprised to hear a car approaching up the hill.

'Who on earth can that be?' wondered Bess, as powerful headlights brushed the window. Then she giggled. 'Perhaps it's the double-glazing salesman,' she said.

'I'll go and see,' volunteered Chris, as a car door slammed in the yard. He got up and ran into the hall; Finn heard him opening the outer door, then a man's deep voice. A moment later Chris was back in the kitchen, looking like an animated exclamation mark. 'It's Mr Aldie,' he announced dramatically.

Finn gasped, but Douglas said, 'Ask him to come in.'

The most surprising thing about Mr Aldie, the boys agreed later, was that he was both good-looking and very like Andrew. This came as a particular shock to Finn, who had imagined him as Count Dracula. A tall, broad-shouldered man with rosy cheeks and floppy, dark red hair, he stood hesitantly in the doorway in his country clothes, looking at the company with shy blue eyes.

'I'm sorry. I'm interrupting your supper,' he said.

Douglas and Bess covered embarrassment with hospitable noises.

'Not at all. We've finished,' Douglas assured him.

'We're just going to have our coffee,' Bess said. 'Please come and sit down. I'll get another cup.'

Finn didn't think Mr Aldie looked keen, but when Chris dragged over an extra chair he sat on it, and when Douglas passed round cups of coffee he accepted one. He rubbed his nose uneasily with a large hand.

Finn decided that he liked the look of Andy's dad.

'Mr Aldie, how is Andrew?' he asked, and Chris echoed anxiously, 'Yes, how is he?'

'He came home this morning,' Mr Aldie told them. 'He's feeling much better, thank you very much.' But then he turned and spoke directly to Colin and Douglas. 'I didn't mean to accept your hospitality,' he said, 'but it's kind of you, considering how you feel about me. I only came to thank you, Mr Cooper, for helping

Andrew out of the well, and to tell you that I've with-drawn my application for permission to dig gravel in the Roman field.'

Six pairs of eyes stared at him in shocked silence. They had been wondering why he had come, but this possibility would never have crossed their minds.

Eventually Granny said gently, 'Is it because of what the Curtises did to Andrew?' and Finn saw Mr Aldie press his hands down on his knees because they were shaking. But he answered Granny calmly.

'Yes,' he said. 'That, on top of other things.'

'Oh, Lord. You mean us, don't you?' said Bess, her small face going pink. 'Because we opposed you.'

'I didn't oppose him,' said Granny indignantly. 'Speak for yourself, Bess Cooper.'

She caught Mr Aldie's eye and they smiled at each other, but Mr Aldie hastened to reassure Bess.

'Not so,' he told her. 'I expected opposition, and I could understand the environmental argument.' His lips curved slightly as he added, 'Goodness knows, I hear it often enough from my twelve-year-old.' But then he continued seriously, 'You opposed me cleanly and fairly, and I could cope with that. But Curtis — well, he was something else.'

He paused, frowning the way Andrew sometimes did when he was puzzled or anxious, and Bess whispered, 'You mean — he did other things?'

Mr Aldie nodded.

'Did them, or incited his boys to do them, which is

far worse. In the past month we've had windows broken and our garden vandalized in the night. I've had my car tyres slashed and my wife's had threatening phone calls. I couldn't prove it was Curtis trying to scare me off, though I knew it was – and now apparently the younger boy has made a confession to the police, blaming the whole thing on his father.' Then, while everyone sat appalled, Mr Aldie said unhappily, 'The worst of it is that I feel guilty, as if my actions have ruined another family.'

There was a murmur of indignant dissent, as Mr Aldie's old opponents went over to his side, and Granny said sparkily, 'Nonsense, young man. We're all responsible for the way we behave. You wanted to provide jobs for unemployed people, and I've been with you all the way.'

Finn knew that this was true. From the beginning, Granny alone had understood that in the business of the gravel pit there weren't heroes and villains, only good people who had different ideas about what mattered most. He could see that Mr Aldie and Granny liked each other a lot. They exchanged smiles again, and Mr Aldie said, 'Well, thanks. I'm glad somebody believed I wasn't a complete crook.' He took a gulp of coffee, and began to explain.

'Three evenings a week, I help to run a club for young unemployed people. They're decent kids, but they have no qualifications, and of course the few jobs available go to youngsters who have. I thought that if I started some enterprise where simple skills could be easily learnt, I could offer employment, at least to some of them.' He smiled, more to himself than to them, then confessed, 'Of course I'd have made money out of it. I'm good at making money. But I wouldn't have carved up the Roman field for gain. Only for people.'

Granny nodded, with an I-told-you-so expression on her face, but there was an uncomfortable silence among the rest. They were finding it hard to equate this nice, kindly man with the greedy, selfish monster they had supposed him to be. Douglas tried to fill the silence by pouring more coffee, and asking if anyone would like a chocolate truffle. Then Mr Aldie went on.

'My wife and I agreed that because we believed in what we were doing, we'd take everything that Curtis threw at us, rather than back down. But that was before we realized how far he would go. After what happened to our boy, there's no way we could risk going ahead. Besides, none of us wants to stay here any longer.' He looked sadly at Chris, and said, 'Andrew's told me how bad he was to you. He's sorry, and so am I. If I'd known, I'd never have suggested he should try to make friends with you.'

Chris went scarlet, but before he could speak, Mr Aldie had turned back to the grown-ups.

'With one thing and another, the boy needs a new start somewhere else, and so does his mother. I'm going to sell up here and look for a house in Strathyre, where my wife has family. But I wish you all well. You're decent folk, and I have no quarrel with you.'

Finn and Chris eyed each other disconsolately, while Bess said, 'Oh, Lord,' and Granny sighed, 'Oh, dearie me.'

But it was Colin, who had sat silent since Mr Aldie entered the room, who began the task of changing his mind.

'I know it's asking a lot,' he said, 'but I do hope you'll think again. I can't pretend Douglas and Bess and I aren't relieved by your decision about the gravel pit, though we respect your reason for wanting it, and it's tough on the kids you wanted to help. But –' he leaned forward and looked intensely at Mr Aldie with his dark brown eyes '– if you pack up now, you'll be going when, for the first time, we have a chance to change Glenaire for the better. Isn't that right, Doug?'

Douglas nodded vigorously.

'Yes,' he agreed. 'The law will punish Curtis, and a good thing too. But what's really important is that the people who blindly followed him are sickened, and don't want any more to do with him. His power here is broken, and suddenly there's a mood for getting together to work out new ways of running things.'

'Won't you stay and help us?' pleaded Bess. 'If we put our heads together, we may even be able to think of something else your young people could do.'

'No more outsiders,' said Finn.

Mr Aldie shook his head as he got to his feet. 'I'll

have to talk to my wife and Andrew,' he said, but there was a thoughtful expression in his eyes which suggested he might be willing to reconsider.

Bess went with Mr Aldie to the door. She said goodnight, and was about to close it when Chris ducked under her arm. In the narrow shaft of light he ran into the yard.

'Mr Aldie,' he called. 'Please, wait!' Mr Aldie stood with his hand on the handle of the car door. Chris leant against the bumper, and words began to tumble out. 'Mr Aldie, tell Andy that me and Finn will come to see him tomorrow. We'll bring a game. And tell him that when he's better, I'll go to Perth pool with him and teach him to swim. It's the only thing I'm good at. And please, don't leave. Who'll be my mate at Muirs High, if you do?'

He could still feel the friendly pressure of Mr Aldie's hand on his shoulder, long after the red tail-lights had disappeared down the hill.

Also by Eileen Dunlop

FINN'S ISLAND

Finn Lochlan's father is a failed teacher, and a failure at farming. Finn is ashamed of him. All Finn can think of with any pride is his grandfather: in particular his stories of life on Hirsay, a remote Scottish island, where life was primitive, but full of adventure, and above all, exciting!

When Finn has the chance to go to Hirsay, he is thrilled. However, events and the weather take a desperate turn for the worse, and Finn discovers the hard way how romantic his ideas of life on Hirsay were . . .

Full of action, and with a strong environmental theme, the story charts Finn's developing relationship with his father as he learns to break with the past and look to the future.

GREEN WILLOW'S SECRET

After the tragic death of her sister Juliet, Kit's family move to Maddimoss. However, Juliet wasn't Kit's real sister: Kit is adopted and guiltily feels glad she no longer has to compete with Juliet.

Bored and alone, Kit starts exploring and finds a photograph of a Japanese garden nearby. Nothing strange about that, except there is a figure in it which appears and disappears . . .

Then Daniel arrives, and together they become entangled in an intriguing mystery. What is the ghostly presence in the garden trying to tell them?